TO EVEN THE ODDS

Slocum reached over and grabbed the rifle riding at Bendix's knee. He swung it around and levered a round into the chamber. When an incautious outlaw stepped out from behind a maple, Slocum drew a bead and fired. The rifle bucked hard against his shoulder but he felt good about the shot. He didn't have to see the outlaw double over and drop to his knees to know he had fired right on target.

"Go!" Slocum shouted. Bendix spurred his tired horse toward Orofino, leaving Slocum in the center of the road. He studied the wooded area where his sniper had been but saw no other outlaws coming out. This told him they were probably going to get their horses and pursue.

Slocum decided to take the fight to Quince.

JAKE LOGAN

SLOCUM

AND THE

BITTERROOT BELLE

JOVE BOOKS, NEW YORK

This is a work of fiction. Names, characters, places, and incidents either
are the product of the author's imagination or are used fictitiously,
and any resemblance to actual persons, living or dead, business
establishments, events, or locales is entirely coincidental.

SLOCUM AND THE BITTERROOT BELLE

A Jove Book / published by arrangement with
the author

PRINTING HISTORY
Jove edition / June 2003

For information address: The Berkley Publishing Group,
a division of Penguin Group (USA) Inc.,
375 Hudson Street, New York, New York 10014.

ISBN: 0-515-13548-8

A JOVE BOOK®
Jove Books are published by The Berkley Publishing Group,
a division of Penguin Group (USA) Inc.,
375 Hudson Street, New York, New York 10014.
JOVE and the "J" design
are trademarks belonging to Penguin Group (USA) Inc.

PRINTED IN THE UNITED STATES OF AMERICA

10 9 8 7 6 5 4 3 2 1

1

"Outlaws? Who gives a damn about outlaws when I got you ridin' at my side, Slocum?" Clint Bendix laughed as he checked his wagon. The rear wheel had turned wobbly a few miles outside Lewiston, Idaho, threatening to delay the supplies they shipped to the mining boomtown of Orofino.

"You'd better," John Slocum said, his green eyes narrowing as he scanned the street. Two suspicious gents loitered across the muddy street trying to make it look like they didn't know each other. They failed. Now and then one lifted a hand to cover his lips and obviously whispered to the man standing next to him. When they saw Slocum eyeing them, they turned and hurried off as if somebody had set fire to their boots. This made Slocum even more suspicious.

"I've heard all them tall tales," Clint said, grunting as he tried to turn the locking nut on the wheel. He readjusted the big wrench he used but still couldn't tighten the nut to keep the wheel from wobbling. "I got bigger problems. This here wheel's got to come off. That means unloading the cargo since there's no way I can jack it up otherwise. Not unless you've got more piss and vinegar in you than I think."

"You shouldn't have let all your mule skinners go get drunk," Slocum said.

"I do declare, Slocum, you got more advice that's worthless than any man I ever heard. If I hadn't told them stinkin' skinners they could quaff a drink or two, they'd've upped and quit on me. This is the first town with decent saloons in it we've seen since we left Seattle. Too danged many Mormons in Coeur d'Alene for decent waterin' holes."

"We're going to need more than their strong backs," Slocum said. "We'll need their shotguns, too."

"There you go again. I heard the rumors of road agents workin' these here byways same as you, but we ain't seen hide nor hair of anyone, much less an outlaw, in the week we've been travelin' from Coeur d'Alene."

"There's supposed to be an entire town filled with outlaws somewhere around here," Slocum said. "The federal marshal hasn't flushed them after more than a year of trying."

"Then there's the Lost Dutchman Mine and the rest of them things that don't exist." Clint laughed heartily. "Imagine a whole danged town filled with crooks and cutthroats. Why, it'd be like going dockside in San Francisco!"

"I'll fetch a few of the teamsters to help you with the wheel," Slocum said. He hitched up the Colt Navy slung in a cross-draw holster at his left side and reluctantly left Clint Bendix to his work. They had six wagons, all crammed with prime luxury goods slated for gold miners. Bendix would turn a fabulous profit with this single shipment that couldn't be matched unless he had brought along six wagons of willing women.

"Go on, Slocum. I kin look after business." Bendix wiped the sweat from his forehead as he studied the wag-

, lined up alongside the road. The one he drove was the only one with any problems, and from the look of it the Lewiston wheelwright might get some business out of it. "All I need do is chase off street urchins pokin' around."

Slocum grunted and cut across the street to the feed and seed store where the men had lingered as they watched Bendix struggle with the busted wheel. He glanced into the store but saw no one. If a clerk had been there, he would have asked after the men to find out what their feigned disinterest in the supply wagons really meant.

His long stride lengthened when he heard a ruckus in the nearest saloon. Slocum stepped away from a plate-glass window in time to avoid the body tossed through it. A buckskin-clad giant of a man landed flat on his back in front of Slocum and lay stunned for a moment. Then he growled like a bear and got to his feet.

"Greene," Slocum said, reaching out and grabbing the man's shoulder to hold him back. "What's going on?"

An even louder growl sounded and Slocum felt a heavy hand shove him aside. The power behind that meaty hand on his shoulder sent him reeling. He regained his balance and went for his six-shooter in time to see a mountain man rearing back over the huge Benny Greens and then letting loose with a powerful punch that lifted the muleteer off his feet. Greene was out cold by the time he fell to the ground a second time.

"Don't *ever* say my Sadie's ugly," panted the man who had knocked out Greene with a single potent blow.

"She's mighty fine-lookin', Hale. Mighty fine-lookin'," said a nervous onlooker when the mountain man spun around looking for assurance he was right. The rest of the men who had rushed from the saloon all nodded in agreement.

"Come on, Greene," Slocum said, grunting as he got

the teamster to a sitting position. Greene mumbled something Slocum didn't understand.

"You his friend?" demanded Hale. He loomed over Slocum like a nightmare, hands balled into fists the size of smoked Virginia hams. He clenched his hands so hard his knuckles cracked.

"We're partners. We work for the same man," Slocum said, not wanting to tangle with the mountain man. Hale looked as if he wrestled bears—and won.

"He insulted my Sadie. If he don't apologize, I'll rip his head off and shit down the bleedin' hole."

"We've been on the trail for a spell," Slocum said, letting Greene flop back onto the ground so he could stand and put a few feet between him and Hale. "He's not used to drinking like he must have done back there. He probably said things he shouldn't have."

Slocum didn't know how Greene could have gotten so drunk so fast, but the mule skinner had done more to rile folks in Lewiston in fifteen minutes than most could do in a week of trying.

"You apologize for him," Hale said.

"He didn't mean to insult your woman," Slocum said. "He—"

Hale let out a roar of anger and charged Slocum so fast that it caught him completely by surprise. Powerful arms circled Slocum's shoulders like steel bands and pinned his arms to his sides. He cried out in pain as Hale began squeezing him in a bear hug that would snap his back like a twig if he didn't get loose quick.

Slocum thrashed about but couldn't win free. He did succeed in getting his right hand over to the ebony butt of his six-gun. But pressed so forcibly against Hale's chest, he could never hope to draw. The best he could do was cock the pistol and fire it while it was still in the holster.

The hot streak of pain down the side of his leg told

Slocum where the bullet had gone. Then the pressure around him suddenly evaporated and Hale bellowed like an angry bull.

"You shot me in the foot. You goddamn shot me in the foot!" The mountain man hopped about, trying to clutch his foot. Blood oozed through the right moccasin, showing that Slocum's shot had found a target other than his own flesh.

"I'm gonna kill you both!" Hale hopped about, trying to come after Slocum and at the same time do something about his bullet-holed foot. As he lumbered over, Slocum judged distances, ignored the pain in his own leg and then kicked as hard as he could.

The toe of his boot crunched into Hale's left kneecap. With his right foot shot through and his left kneecap broken, Hale tumbled to the ground like a felled tree. He rolled around, screaming at the top of his lungs and lunging for anyone foolish enough to get close. Rabid dogs were easier to deal with than the injured giant.

Slocum took three quick steps away and turned so his bloody thigh was hidden from sight as the sheriff shoved through the crowd. Badge shining in the bright Idaho sun, the lawman planted himself squarely in front of Hale and then reached down to grab the man by the front of his buckskins. With a mighty heave, the sheriff lifted Hale to his feet.

"You were warned," the sheriff said, grabbing a handful of hair to hold Hale's head in place. "I told you not to disturb the peace no more. You get the hell out of town. You got ten minutes, Hale. If I see one greasy hair of yours anywhere in Lewiston after that, I'll throw your whole damned head into jail. And I might not put the rest of your body in the same cell!" The sheriff shoved Hale back and then wiped his hand off on his vest.

He swung around and faced the crowd. His voice crackled and snapped like mountain thunder.

"No fightin' in my town. I've been sheriff of Nez Perce County for a month now, and there ain't been a single murder. That's the way it's gonna stay, too, or my name's not Gerald P. Allen!" He glared at the crowd until they began fading away to return to their drinking. This time they had plenty to talk about over their nickel beers and two-bit shots of trade whiskey.

Hale shuffled off, grumbling insults as he went, but Allen turned his attention to Slocum.

"You the one who fired the shot?"

"Did more damage to myself than I did to him," Slocum allowed, jerking his thumb in the direction of the slowly retreating mountain man to keep the sheriff from seeing the bloody gash on the side of his leg. Slocum was still alive, and that's what mattered, but it was mighty embarrassing for a man to shoot himself in a fight.

"I don't cotton much to shootin' up the town, but he came after you. I saw it from down the street, as I stepped from my office. What'd you say to get Hale so riled? He's not a peaceable fellow even when he's sober, but I never saw him that mad."

"I was trying to soothe ruffled feathers. My friend there on the ground must have insulted Hale's woman."

"Woman?" The sheriff looked puzzled.

"Naw wamn," muttered Greene, fighting to sit up again. "Mool."

"I don't—" started Slocum.

"He said, he wasn't insulting Hale's woman. That galoot's not gotten laid in a month of Sundays, since even Lewiston's whores have better taste. You must have said something bad about his mule."

Greene's head bobbed in assent, then he blanched under his weather-beaten exterior and grabbed for his jaw.

"Better get him to Doc Dawson. He's not a people doctor but he fixes up animals pretty good. Think your partner's got a busted jaw."

Before Slocum could ask Sheriff Allen about the two men who had been watching Clint Bendix's wagons, the lawman cried out and rushed into the saloon to break up another fight. Slocum would have followed, but Greene let out another moan of stark pain.

"Come on. Let's find the vet and see if he can get your jaw wired up," Slocum said, heaving Greene to his feet. "Looks like you're going to be drinking your meals for a spell."

The animal noise Greene made sounded as if he thought he could live for a month or two on nothing but whiskey. For all Slocum knew, maybe Greene could. After all, he was a mule driver—but not one who was going to drive Bendix's wagons to Orofino.

Slocum found the veterinarian's office and guided Greene to a sturdy table that could have held a small calf and might have at some point.

"Whatcha got there? Hmm, busted jaw," the doctor said. Dawson peered over his reading glasses at Slocum and asked, "You payin' for me to fix him up? He's in no condition to agree to anything, not with his jaw like that."

"I'll pay," Slocum said. To Greene he said, "I'll see that Bendix takes it out of your pay."

This produced a loud grunt of complaint that turned to pain as Dr. Dawson began probing to find the extent of the damage. Slocum watched in admiration. He had seen medical doctors with less skill. It took the better part of an hour before Greene was all wired up like a champagne bottle.

"Let me look at your leg," Dawson said. "That's a nasty cut you got." He peered through his glasses at the wound, then made a face. "Gunshot."

"No fooling," Slocum said, wincing as the doctor poured carbolic acid on the wound. With skill equaling that he had already shown, Dawson patched up Slocum's leg.

"Be good as new in a week. Keep the bandage dry. If you don't, be sure to change it for something that's not entirely filthy."

"Thanks, Doc," Slocum said. "Anything I can do for you, let me know."

"Bring me some business," the vet said. "There's so danged much rustling going on, the cows don't have a chance to get sick so I can overcharge their owners to cure them."

"That why you're so good at fixing up human wounds?" asked Slocum.

"A man's got to stay alive. I prefer animals, but I'll go slumming if I have to and mend a two-legged varmint, as long as he can pay."

Slocum paid for him and Greene, then left.

"Gddby," muttered Greene. He shoved out a beefy hand. Slocum understood and shook it.

"It'll take Bendix a while longer to fix the wagon. Come by and get the rest of your pay."

"Sloon," Greene said.

"I got it. You'll be in the saloon. Don't cross any more mountain men, and if you do, be sure to compliment their mules." Slocum slapped Greene on the shoulder, watched the man wince with the impact, then turned and went back to the wagons to give Clint Bendix the bad news. He either had to hire a new muleteer or leave a wagon behind.

As Slocum neared the wagons, he saw they had been left unguarded. The wagon with the broken wheel was propped up on a rock, but Bendix was nowhere to be seen and at the last wagon were the two men Slocum had spotted earlier. They had thrown back the tattered canvas covering the crates of sardines, cases of champagne and iced-down oysters and were rooting about in the wagon itself.

Slocum slid his six-shooter from its holster and started for the men. Something warned them, because they popped up like prairie dogs and jumped to the ground.

"Stop!" Slocum called, breaking into a clumsy run. His leg hurt him enough to slow down his rush or he might have caught them.

The two men crammed papers into their shirts and ran like the wind, heads down to keep from revealing their faces until they reached the corner of a bakery. One looked back, so Slocum got a quick look at him. Then they skidded around the building and vanished. By the time Slocum limped over, the pair was long gone.

He slammed his Colt Navy back into his holster, wondering what the hell was going on since neither of the men had tried to steal anything from the wagon.

2

"What's wrong, Slocum?" called Clint Bendix, coming up rolling a wheel. "You got the look of somebody givin' your tail a real twist."

"Everything's all right," Slocum said, checking the wagon where the two men had been poking around. He found nothing missing. He frowned, though, when he saw the canvas untied on the other five wagons. The men had spent a considerable time looking for something but hadn't bothered stealing so much as a bottle of champagne.

"Give me a hand, will you? I was lucky gettin' this wheel out of the blacksmith. Drove a hard bargain, he did, but time's a-wastin' since I want to get everything to Orofino before the oysters turn bad and the champagne corks pop from the heat. Heard tell there's a big gold strike."

"How long do you think it'll take us?" asked Slocum.

"Two days, no more, if we drive like sons-a-bitches. Then I'll be rich and you and the rest of the crew can share in it."

"Yeah, rich," Slocum said, fastening the last of the canvas flaps back into place. He put his back into lifting as

10

Bendix positioned the wheel on the bare axle and moved it into place. It took less than a minute to spin the nut back on and tighten it down with the wrench he had stashed in the wagon bed.

"Round up the rest of the muleteers and get the teams hitched. We can get most of the way to Orofino and then roll into town bright and early day after tomorrow."

"There's been a bit of trouble," Slocum said, explaining how they had lost Benny Greene as a driver. "You want to hire someone? From the look of the drunks at the saloon, you'll have your choice of drivers."

Clint Bendix pursed his lips and shook his shaggy head. He started to speak, then clamped his mouth shut as he rubbed his stubbled chin, obviously thinking hard. When he looked up at Slocum, what he wanted was as plain as day.

"John, could you drive a wagon? Double pay. Driver and guard. That's five percent of the gross sales for you."

Slocum did a quick calculation and decided he might see as much as a thousand dollars. He had nursemaided the wagon train all the way from Seattle, but it had been easy work. The vaunted outlaws had never shown their ugly faces, and the only troubles had been wagons breaking down. The broken wheel was only the latest of the damage the rough roads had done to the decrepit wagons Bendix had bought out on the Pacific Coast.

"That's mighty generous," Slocum said.

"Speed getting to Orofino counts fer everything. I tell you, the 'smith said the gold strike there's caused one huge boom. Miners are flockin' in like famished locusts on a wheat field. Millionaires are made overnight. I want some of that gold 'fore the gamblers and other swindlers take it from those hard rock fools."

Slocum considered the goods Bendix was shipping and knew he was right. If the gold strike was anywhere near what it sounded, anyone giving the lucky miners what they needed to celebrate would get rich.

"Done," Slocum said, thrusting out his hand. Clint Bendix shook hard and grinned his broken-toothed grin.

"Knew I could count on you, Slocum. Now quit lollygaggin' and let's get the mule skinners in their boxes and movin' on down the road!"

Slocum spent the next half hour rounding up the muleteers, feeling like a cowboy lassoing strays. How the men had gotten as drunk as they had so quickly was a mystery to him, but their level of inebriation seemed to have no effect on their skill in getting the balky mules moving along the road at a steady clip.

Although it had been a goodly while since he had driven a team, Slocum found the habits came back quick. The twenty-foot-long whip uncurled and cracked directly over the long ears of the lead mule and kept it pulling, even when they reached a steep slope that required maximum effort.

For more than three hours they made good progress, and then Slocum began to feel uneasy. Driving required most of his attention, but he caught sight of riders out of the corner of his eyes. Every time, though, when he turned to get a better look, the horsemen vanished as if they were nothing more than smoke in a high wind.

"Bendix!" Slocum called. "Rein back. We got problems!"

"Damn," he heard the wagon master curse. Slocum knew how eager Bendix was to get his cargo to Orofino, but the man had sense enough to stand, shove his boot against his brake and push hard on it as he tugged on the mules' reins.

Slocum quickly stopped his wagon, secured the reins and hopped down to walk to the lead wagon.

"What is it?" demanded Bendix. "We got a rough section of road comin' up. I feel it in my bones."

"I'm not wasting time," Slocum said. "There are out-riders paralleling our path fifty yards away. Let me see what they're up to before we go on."

"No!"

"Bendix, you were the one who worried about outlaws all the way across Idaho. Those riders might be scouts sizing us up." Slocum looked at the other drivers. Most had sobered up during the last hour or two but one mule skinner still looked drunker than a lord. Slocum guessed he had brought a bottle of whiskey along to keep him company on a dry, dusty trip.

None of them would put up much of a fight if it came to shooting.

"We outrun them. There's no point in you gettin' your-self killed tryin' to find who's out there. We leave 'em in the dust. Get back there to your rig and let's drive!" Ben-dix shouted out encouragement as he let his brake slip free and used the blacksnake whip to get his mules pulling again.

Slocum shook his head. The men spying on the wagons had disappeared like smoke, but Slocum knew there would be trouble. As surely as Bendix felt the lay of the land and the way the road would turn rough, Slocum felt the danger crackling all around like the air before a light-ning strike. He climbed into the driver's box, made sure his Winchester was handy and then concentrated on guid-ing his team on the smoothest part of the road, if one rock under the wheel could be considered smaller than any other.

They had driven less than a mile when disaster struck. Slocum heard rather than saw the axle on Bendix's wagon snap. He drove around a bend in the road and then reined back, giving the mules a needed rest.

"Dangnabit," grumbled Clint Bendix, already crouching down to look at the rear axle. "The wood must not have been cured right. Axle started to bow, from the look of it, then snapped when I hit a pothole."

"We've got a spare," Slocum pointed out.

"But the time!" moaned the wagon master. "It'll take us damned near till sundown to change axles. That's valuable time lost."

"So we're a day later than we figured," Slocum said, trying to put the best face on the problem. "We get into Orofino at sundown instead of sunrise."

Bendix grumbled, then shrugged off his sorry fate.

"Heard tell there's a shebang somewhere along the trail. No reason we can't reach it and give the teams a good feeding. Might push 'em faster tomorrow and still get to Orofino on schedule."

"Could be," Slocum allowed. He knew the only schedule rode in Bendix's mind. One day, more or less, meant nothing. He had checked the ice on the oysters and they could spend the next couple days getting to Orofino and still have living, salable oysters for the luxury-starved miners.

The muleteers that weren't suffering as badly as the others from the vile trade whiskey they had swilled in Lewiston pitched in to swap the busted axle with one carried in Slocum's wagon. Considering all the factors, Slocum thought they had worked quickly and well, but Bendix carped about running behind his precious timetable.

They rolled out warily, the sun setting behind the distant hills and bringing a chill to the land. What worried Slocum more than the cold was his inability to see the shadow-hidden road well enough to avoid hitting every chuckhole and jagged rock. Still, he maintained the furious pace set by Clint Bendix until they reached a mountain meadow.

Slocum spotted the shebang mentioned by Bendix right away. The modest caravansary looked like an oasis to him. A tall brick chimney let curls of smoke escape, bringing the savory scent of stew cooking over a fire. Stables behind the shebang promised care for the mules. Slocum smiled. Bendix might even be able to trade some of his goods for a spare axle, as insurance against the increasingly rough road leading into Orofino.

"Looks to be a good place to spend the night," Bendix shouted back. He wiped his lips and Slocum knew he had caught the smell of fresh stew, too. No one in the company cooked worth a damn, and after the last day or two, they could all use a decent meal. Maybe one cooked by the owner's wife or daughter. Female companionship might prove to be a source of trouble among the mule skinners, but Slocum knew he and Bendix were up to keeping order.

It might take Bendix offering the teamsters a bottle or two of his precious champagne, but it would be worth it.

As they brought their wagons to a halt, Slocum got a better look at the stables and wondered at the horses kept there. The only riders he had seen along the road were those who had spied on them just outside Lewiston. A quick count told him at least ten horses—none of them with the look of a draft animal—were corraled out back.

Slocum shrugged it off. Men who ran establishments like this often fancied themselves to be horse traders.

"You boys settle down out here while me and Slocum see what they can do fer us."

"I want *two* plates of that stew," called a mule skinner.

"What's wrong, Pete? Ain't ya hungry?" joked another. "I'll take *three*!"

Slocum and Bendix walked to the front door of the shebang. The paint had peeled and the place looked shabbier than Slocum had originally thought. If he tried to lean against a wall, the entire structure might fall down. He wondered what else the gathering twilight hid.

"Howdy, gents." They were greeted by a burly man

who filled the entire doorway with his bulk. The first thing Slocum noticed was the six-gun slung at the man's hip. A legitimate hotelier out in the backwoods might carry a gun, but not slung gunfighter fashion. The worn leather holster said that six-shooter had seen hard and heavy use.

Without realizing it, Slocum moved his own hand a shade closer to his Colt.

"Evening," Clint Bendix said. "Me and my boys'd like to spend the night. If we could sample some of that stew you got cookin', we'd be mighty appreciative."

"Reckon you would," the man said. Something about his arrogant tone put Slocum even more on edge, but Bendix didn't notice.

"If you have grain and maybe a carrot or two fer my teams, that'd be real good, too," Bendix went on. He was oblivious to the trouble mounting until he looked into the main room and saw three men reaching for shotguns.

"What's going on?" Bendix asked. He stepped back and bumped into Slocum. "Why are those men goin' fer their guns?"

"Now, that's a good question and one you can answer."

"You're thieves," Bendix said. "Road agents!"

"You got that wrong, mister," the man said. "In fact, you got it exactly backwards."

"What are you tryin' to say?" Bendix had finally figured out how much trouble they were in.

Slocum reached for his six-shooter but froze when he heard a rifle hammer cocking behind him. He glanced over his shoulder and saw three more men, all with Winchesters leveled at him and Bendix.

"What I'm saying is pretty obvious. We ain't crooks. *You're* the owlhoots who stole *my* property."

"I don't follow you," Slocum said. He let his hand drift away from the butt of his six-shooter. He didn't want to get ventilated because one of the riflemen thought he was trying to throw down on the shebang owner.

"Reckon you'd play it stupid. Jed," the man called. "You got the rest of them varmints all rounded up?"

"Surely do, Quince. They didn't put up a fight. Cowards, the lot of them. Just like you said, yellow-bellied sneak thieves."

"Now look here," started Bendix. The man called Quince whipped out his six-shooter and buffaloed the wagon master. The crack of metal against the side of Bendix's head made Slocum turn cold inside. He looked at the ground where Bendix moaned as he clutched his bleeding scalp.

"You have us confused with somebody else," Slocum said in a level voice. He waited for a chance to get the drop on Quince, although that might not stop the rest from filling him full of lead.

"Don't think so. I've been havin' all my supplies stolen. I pay for them, only to have some clever thief make off with them." Quince holstered his pistol, then dug around in his shirt pocket before pulling out a few sheets of paper.

"What's that?" asked Bendix, blood oozing between his fingers as he pressed his hand to his cut scalp.

"You wouldn't recognize these," Quince said, sneering. "They're receipts. Bills of sale, all made out to me for what you got in those wagons."

"I bought everything in Seattle!"

"Don't know what you did in Seattle. These here receipts say I bought six wagons filled with luxury goods in Coeur d'Alene. Had hardly loaded the crates when you stole it all. I ought to string you up."

"You're wrong," Slocum said, but a cold lump in his belly told him they had walked into a clever swindle.

"Let's check to see how close my receipts match what you owlhoots have loaded in them wagons." Quince swaggered out, Slocum and Bendix following. Behind them trailed six gunmen, all alert for any move on Slocum's part.

The teamsters working for Bendix had been herded away from the wagons and were under guard of a pair of shotgun-toting men.

"We couldn't stop 'em, Bendix. We tried but—" The teamster got a shotgun barrel alongside his head for his trouble.

"That's all right, boys. We'll take care of this," Bendix said, anger smoldering. "Go on. Check your list and you'll see it doesn't match what I got."

Slocum wasn't a bit surprised when wagon after wagon matched the bill of lading Quince clutched in his beefy hand.

"Yep, this is my shipment, all paid for and officially documented," Quince finished, waving the papers under Bendix's nose. "Now, I have never been too friendly with the law, so if you folks just mosey on out, I won't turn you over to the marshal."

"You won't turn *us* over?" Clint Bendix sputtered angrily.

"Come on," Slocum said, taking the merchant by the arm and pulling him away. "Let's get out of here before they take it into their heads to kill us all."

"We'd have to shoot you if you tried anything," Quince said, grinning wolfishly.

"The wagons are mine!" Bendix cried.

"Nope, you stole them, too. And the mule teams."

"Not the horse," Slocum said. "That's nowhere on your receipt." He pointed to his saddle horse. Quince hurriedly pawed through the bogus list and then sneered.

"Go on, take it. Six of you can't ride one horse."

Slocum silently saddled his horse, started to take his Winchester from the wagon and found himself staring down the double barrels of a shotgun, then left his rifle. He climbed into the saddle and led the sorry parade of Clint Bendix and four muleteers back onto the road alongside the shebang.

"Which way?" Slocum asked. "Back to Lewiston or on to Orofino?"

Clint Bendix was so furious he foamed at the mouth. He pointed in the direction of Orofino and managed to croak out, "Closer. Orofino's closer. The sooner we bring the law back here, the sooner I get my merchandise back from those no-account road agents!"

Slocum wasn't so sure but turned his horse's face in the direction of the boomtown.

3

Footsore and getting angrier with every step, Clint Bendix entered Orofino chewing nails and spitting tacks. Slocum rode alongside slowly, turning over in his mind everything that had happened to them back at the shebang. He had crossed some clever road agents in his day, but Quince had come up with a new way of stealing.

It seemed almost legal.

Slocum just wished he had stopped the two men back in Lewiston before they had taken such a detailed inventory of everything Bendix had carried in his wagons. Without the list, Quince would have found himself in a position of either taking the supplies at gunpoint or arguing the matter in front of a lawman. As it was, Slocum held out little hope that Bendix would convince anyone he was the legitimate owner of everything in the six wagons.

"You boys just go get likkered up," Bendix said, fumbling in his pocket and tossing each of the four muleteers a silver cartwheel. "When I get things squared away, I'll need you to drive them wagons back into town."

"Clint, I like you and all," spoke up Pete, "but I ain't

walkin' back to the wagons. My feet ain't seen this much ground since Hector was a pup."

"You'll ride back in style. I swear it," Bendix said. For a moment Slocum almost believed it. Then the wagon master spotted the town marshal and rushed off to present his case.

Slocum was slower to follow, not wanting to muddy the waters with a lot of pointless questions the lawman was likely to ask. Why Slocum had been allowed to keep his horse would be high on the list of things not needing to be answered and would certainly occur to even the densest marshal.

As Slocum dismounted and overheard part of what Clint Bendix said, he wondered if he had overestimated the lawman.

"I can't do a danged thing for you, Mr. Bendix," the marshal said. "If'n Mr. Quince's got a receipt for all that merchandise, then it's his. I mean, it might not be his but he can prove it is."

"I've got receipts, too!" shouted Bendix. "Telegraph my suppliers in Seattle. They'll tell you."

"Reckon I could do that, if I had a mind," the marshal said, sucking on his gums. "Then again, what if I telegraphed Coeur d'Alene and the supplier there said Quince had bought all that stuff? Where'd that leave me?"

"Marshal," Slocum said, deciding it was time to get involved. "Have any other merchants had the same problem?"

"What problem's that?" asked the lawman ingenuously. Slocum knew Bendix was in a world of trouble then and would never get his wares back.

"You damned fool," raged Bendix. "Have any other merchants complained that Quince stole their supplies!"

"Don't go insultin' me, mister," the marshal said coldly. "I'm the law in Orofino and I don't know you from Adam. Quince, now, he's been around a spell. He and his boys come to town and spend good money. Hard money. The saloon owners appreciate the fact that none of Quince's boys bust up their establishments much. When they do, he's always quick to pay."

"I'll pay if my mule skinners—" Bendix cut off his tirade, sputtering into incoherence.

"Might it be that Quince has so many men in his gang that you're afraid of them?" asked Slocum.

"You button that lip, too, mister," the marshal said. He swallowed hard when he saw he wasn't going to push Slocum around. The marshal hitched up his gun belt, trying to bolster his courage. All he did was look more foolish.

"Quince owns the town, doesn't he?" asked Bendix.

"He just blowed into the area a few weeks back. He don't own Orofino and he don't own me," the marshal said firmly.

"You want to ride out to his shebang so we can discuss the matter at length?" asked Slocum. He read the answer long before the marshal worked out the right way of telling Slocum what he already knew.

"My jurisdiction don't go that far. I'm a town marshal, not a federal marshal. You might talk to the sheriff. The entire county's his province, 'cept in towns like this." The marshal made a vague gesture around his domain. Orofino looked like all the other boom towns Slocum had seen. A dozen saloons lined the main street, the walls crooked and threatening to topple at any moment because they had been put up so fast. Other businesses were crammed in wherever they would fit, and in some cases where they didn't. Doors that ought to have been squared off were canted at odd angles and nobody cared.

The busiest place that Slocum could see was a small assay office down the street, sandwiched between two-story saloons. The line of miners out into the street told him that the rumor of a big gold strike was probably true.

Each of the miners clutched bags to his chest and looked around furtively, waiting to see if anyone intended to jump his claim.

"So you won't help me get my merchandise back?" asked Bendix. The merchant was red in the face now and balled his hands into tight fists. Slocum had seen springs wound up this tight and didn't want to be around when Bendix released all his pent-up anger.

"Your word against his," the marshal said. "Can't say I'd believe him over you, but then there's no reason to say I'd go the other way, either."

"There's nothing like being decisive," Slocum said sarcastically.

"Marshal!" called a man dressed in canvas pants and a ragged wool shirt. "Marshal Watkins! Come quick. There's a big dispute startin' in the White Elephant Saloon!"

"Duty calls, gents," Marshal Watkins said. He nodded in their direction and hurried off before either Slocum or Bendix could say another word.

"If that don't beat all," groused Bendix. "You reckon he's in cahoots with Quince?"

"I doubt it. He doesn't have the spine for the job, that's all," Slocum said.

"Then it's up to us, you and me, Slocum. We have to get back the supplies in those wagons. We can't depend on the teamsters. That means—"

"Whoa, hold on," Slocum interrupted. "Did you count how many men were backing Quince up?"

"Six, eight, what's the difference? We can get my goods out of there. Sneak in, like Indians, see, then drive those wagons out 'fore they know what's happenin'."

Clint Bendix had always been a dreamer but this pipe dream included a serious dose of stupid with it. A small army might pry loose the supplies, but there'd be a whale of a lot of bloodshed getting to that point.

"So we sneak in. If there's only the pair of us, that means we can only get two wagons out." Slocum saw reality crash into Bendix's plan and bring him to a rattling halt.

"We can't let him steal my goods, Slocum. We can't!"

"Quince has done this before," Slocum said. "The operation was slicker than goose shit on glass. That means other people around Orofino—maybe a lot of them—have been robbed in the same way. Why don't you go around and talk to the merchants and find out?"

"There's the owner of the mercantile," Bendix said, pointing to a man wearing an apron, intent on sweeping off the rickety boards in front of a general store. "I can smell 'em a mile off. It's the way they walk, how they look."

"Go talk to him. I'll see what I can scare up in the saloon." Slocum's cold gaze fixed on the White Elephant down the street, next to the land and assay office.

"We can get the cargo back," Bendix said more to himself than Slocum. "I know we can. I ain't lettin' that lowdown snake steal my goods. No, sir." Clint Bendix almost ran across the street to accost the store owner.

Slocum hitched up his gun belt and followed the marshal to the gin mill. He paused in the doorway, noticing they hadn't bothered to put up a door. There weren't even hinges showing a door had once swung here but had been knocked off in some brawl. He reckoned the White Elephant never closed and didn't need a door. If it had been built recently, if the ramshackle construction could be called being built, then the structure hadn't gone through an Idaho winter.

By the time the first snows came whistling down from Canada, Orofino might not even exist. The veins of gold might have petered out and sent all the miners scurrying off to find the next big strike.

Slocum stepped inside and looked around. He saw the

trouble that Marshal Watkins had come to deal with. The
lawman sat with his back to the room, a poker hand in
front of him. A half-empty rye whiskey bottle was close
by, being passed around by the others in the game. When
it came to Watkins, he downed more than his share, wiped
his lips and then continued with betting on what Slocum
guessed was a punk hand.

But the marshal occasionally glanced over his shoulder,
as if worrying that someone sneaked up on him. Slocum
wondered why the man had settled down to play poker
with his back to the door if that bothered him. He let his
eyes cross the busy saloon to the bar and knew right away
what intrigued Watkins so. Slocum couldn't help staring
a little himself.

The barkeep was about the prettiest woman he had seen
in a long time. She was short, petite and had hair the color
of midnight. Her bright blue eyes sparkled as they worked
up and down the bar, appraising each and every patron's
wallet and how much more cheap booze it would take
before he was tapped out.

Slocum pushed his way through the crowded room and
insinuated himself at the far end of the bar where he could
watch the marshal and, coincidentally he told himself, the
pretty bartender.

He had barely sidled in when she spotted him and came
over like an hungry eagle going after a rabbit. Slocum
had never appreciated the feeling of being hunted. Until
now.

"You're new in town," she said. "The name's Jane."

"John Slocum," he said, touching the brim of his hat.
"It's not possible, is it?"

"What's that, John Slocum?" she asked, taken off stride
by his question.

"That every woman in Orofino is as pretty as the barkeep in the White Elephant," he said.

"A gentleman quick with the compliment. From the accent, I'd say a gentleman from Georgia."

Slocum returned her bright smile and said, "I'm from Georgia."

"Ah, I hear a hint of homesickness there. You look as if you've been out west a spell, though."

Slocum said nothing about that. He had fought alongside Quantrill and Bloody Bill Anderson during the war, but had protested the Lawrence, Kansas, raid where the raiders killed every male, no matter if they were six or sixty. For his concern, Slocum had been gut-shot and left to die. After months of painful recovery he had returned to Slocum's Stand, the finest farm in all of Georgia.

But it wasn't as it had been before the war. His parents were dead, his brother Robert had died during Pickett's Charge, and a carpetbagger judge had taken a fancy to the land. When the judge and his hired gun had come out to seize the property for unpaid back taxes, Slocum had not argued.

Instead, he had left two fresh graves near the springhouse up on the hill and gone west.

He missed Georgia and his birthright but not the judge-killing charges that had dogged his steps since.

"Ah, a quiet one. I like that in a man," Jane said. "Let me guess your pleasure."

Slocum's eyes widened in surprise, then he burst out laughing.

"That's easy enough to do, but you probably can't guess what I'd like to drink."

It was Jane's turn to laugh. She reached under the bar and poured three fingers of an amber liquor into a nearly clean shot glass.

"Try that. For a start," she said. The saucy dark-haired woman turned and flounced off, treating him to a sight he hadn't witnessed in too long.

Slocum sipped at his drink and discovered a smooth

whiskey that didn't have the kick of a mule.

"Like it?" Jane shouted from the far end of the bar.

"Billy Taylor's?" he asked, his voice cutting through the drone of the customers. Jane nodded vigorously, blew him a kiss and began a trip down the bar, refilling glasses, flirting with the customers and then moving on quickly until she again ended up in front of him.

"You've got a connoisseur's tongue," she said.

"I'm not exactly sure what that is, but if you say so, it's got to be true."

Jane laughed again and it sounded like wind in the pines, water gushing in a brook, the soft sigh of snow against a windowpane.

"You're keeping a sharp eye on the marshal. Are you on the run or do you want something from him?" Jane poured another drink before Slocum could answer, took the glass from his fingers, then downed the bourbon herself. "Somebody's done you wrong," she decided. She refilled the glass, letting him keep it, but her fingers brushed against his.

Slocum explained what had happened at Quince's shebang and the lack of response he and Bendix had gotten from the marshal.

"Doesn't surprise me much," Jane said. "I've heard most others in town complain about Quince. I've only been here a couple weeks, but there's not a merchant in the area that's not had the same trick played on 'im."

"Is Watkins crooked and in cahoots with Quince or is he just a coward?"

"Could be both, though I'm leaning toward the latter," Jane said. "Hardly ever seen him sober. He'd be one of the best customers in the house, if he ever paid. The boss keeps him in booze because he thinks having the marshal drink here holds down trouble. It doesn't."

"The merchants Quince has stolen from," Slocum said.

"Would they be willing to form a posse and go after him?"

"It'd take a strong man to lead them. That's the problem in Orofino. Weak law, greedy miners, nobody else willing to stick out his neck. Unless you're volunteering to lead the posse. Are you strong enough, John?"

Their eyes locked, his green boring into her dazzling ice-blue ones.

"Yep, I reckon you are," Jane said after a few seconds. "Let me ask around and see how many I can find who'd ride with you."

4

"This is the way it shoulda been done a long time back," Clint Bendix said, looking at the dozen men gathered for the ride out to Quince's shebang to get back the stolen merchandise. "It took a little prodding on my part, but now we're movin'!"

Slocum said nothing about riding with the posse—or should he call it a vigilante group? He felt uneasy that the men had formed so quickly. Such justice usually turned into a necktie party, and he had been at the wrong end of a rope more than once. Escape had been as much a matter of luck as ability more often than not, and had nothing to do with truth.

He knew Quince and his gang were guilty, but loosing vigilantes in a boomtown meant nothing but trouble. Slocum considered how quickly he could move on after Bendix got his goods back. Staying around to see how the taste of power affected these men wasn't anything Slocum looked forward to.

"There's no such critter as a good receipt, not in Quince's hands!" shouted the owner of the Orofino general store. "He's stolen his last shipment!"

"Let's go get 'em!" chimed in Bendix. He put his heels

29

to a horse borrowed from the livery owner, who rode with the posse.

Slocum galloped until he rode knee to knee with Bendix and shouted to him over the thunder of their horses' hooves.

"Can you control them?"

"Do I want to?" Bendix said. "I'm surprised at you, Slocum. You never had much good to say about the law before. Why stop these stout fellows if they're bringin' lawless owlhoots to justice?"

"Mobs turn quick," Slocum said. He had seen vigilantes run out of men to string up and turn on themselves, chewing and gnawing like a wolf with its leg caught in a steel trap. It wasn't pretty what they did to former allies. The fact that Slocum and Bendix and the four muleteers who had reached Orofino with them were outsiders put them in jeopardy. It didn't matter that nobody in Orofino had been there for more than a handful of months.

The mule skinners were the newcomers. That made them targets.

"You worry too much, Slocum," Bendix said. "We kin root out them bastards and do the entire territory some good if we do string 'em up. They stole my teams, don't forget. That makes 'em as bad as horse thieves. Nobody cottons to horse thieves."

Slocum remembered the rifles held in confident hands. Riding up to the roadhouse and demanding the return of the six wagons was a prescription for lead flying. Of the vigilantes, only two or three might return fire. The rest would show the white feather and be back at their favorite Orofino saloon knocking back beer and whiskey before the last gunshot faded away.

As he rode, Slocum wondered about the pretty barkeep. Jane had been more than willing to rustle up the men for the posse and had advised him to ignore Marshal Watkins. The latter advice struck Slocum as decent enough, but her eagerness to get men killed bothered him. That might be what passed for entertainment in town, but Slocum thought of it more as a way to reduce the number of customers at the White Elephant Saloon. No matter if they were successful or not, fewer men would return to Orofino than rode out.

"What's the plan?" Slocum asked.

"Ain't got one," Bendix said. "None other than we ride on up, demand the return of my wagons and anything else Quince has stolen from the good people of Orofino. If they turn over the goods, then we string 'em up. If they don't, we shoot 'em and take what's rightly mine—ours."

Slocum considered riding on to Lewiston and forgetting the promised pay for his work with Clint Bendix. His life meant more to him than a pocket filled with gold eagles. But Bendix was his friend and he had agreed to protect the shipment. In that, he had failed and owed it to Bendix to recover the merchandise. He just wished he was in charge of the vigilantes so it could be done right. The last thing in the world they ought to do was ride in straight-away and put all their cards on the table for Quince to see.

"He's workin' a sweet deal, I'll give the varmint that," Bendix said almost appreciatively, as if he wished he had thought of it first. "He steals merchandise going into Orofino, then sells it at twice the going rate to the merchants. They can't get their wagon trains in since the ones Quince doesn't swindle get shot to hell and gone."

"That ought to tell you how well organized Quince and his gang are," Slocum said. His horse was beginning to falter from the hard galloping. He slowed the pace and saw that the rest of the posse did, also, instinctively look-ing to him to lead them.

"Gather round, men!" shouted Clint Bendix. "We got to plan our attack."

Slocum looked at the stocky merchant and wondered if

anything he had said to Bendix had penetrated. He hoped Bendix had a real plan. Then Slocum saw that all that Bendix wanted was his wares returned.

"We rest our horses a spell," Bendix said, "so they don't look all tuckered out. We got to ride tall in the saddle and look tough when we go to that shebang. Then we call out Quince and demand that he return all my stuff."

"And mine!" called out the owner of the town mercantile.

"Mine, too," spoke up another, who nervously pushed spectacles up on his nose with a shaky hand. Slocum judged the lot and found them wanting.

"He won't give in that easy, Bendix," said Slocum. "You'd better be ready for gunplay."

This sent a ripple through the vigilantes. They had been caught up in the horse race to the shebang and this threw cold water on their fever. Several exchanged glances and would have left then and there if it hadn't been for Bendix and his fiery talk.

"They'll turn tail and run like rabbits when they see the whole damned town is comin' for 'em," insisted Bendix, giving Slocum a look of disapproval. "Get your hoglegs out and let's get 'em!"

Slocum slipped the leather keeper from the hammer of his six-shooter but hung back as the rest of the mob waved their guns in the air. They were more of a danger to themselves than to any of Quince's men. Bendix got the vigilantes moving down the road to the shebang.

Again Slocum caught the smell of cooking stew. If Quince used that as bait to entice travelers, it worked. His belly grumbled at the smell, reminding him how long it had been since he'd eaten a decent meal. Then all thought of food vanished.

Clint Bendix trotted up to the front door and shouted,

"Get your ass out here right now, Quince! We're here to dispense some justice!"

Slocum stood in his stirrups, drew and fired in a smooth motion. His horse shied just enough to send his bullet off a true course, but the lead did kick up a bit of wood off the shebang's roof. The rifleman, who'd been seen by none of the vigilantes save Slocum, jerked as the bullet sang past him, slipped and fell off the steeply pitched roof.

The rest of Quince's gang poked out from behind a couple Douglas fir trees and opened fire. Slocum emptied his six-gun but saw it did nothing to stop the fusillade. Three more men stationed behind bigtooth maples to one side of the shebang opened up with shotguns. They were out of range but enough of the pellets reached their targets to spook horses and nick vigilantes. Either injury was enough to cause the posse to disintegrate.

Horses reared and men screamed in fear and pain. Slocum doubted any of the vigilantes were badly hurt, but they were scared out of their wits. It took less than a minute for them to mill about, then find the road back to Orofino. Slocum hadn't thought it was possible but most of the men returned to town faster than they had left.

Only Bendix, two others and Slocum remained.

Slocum was working to knock out the cylinder in his Colt Navy and replace it with a loaded one when Quince shouted to them from inside the roadhouse, "You boys give it up now. We won't kill you. Might have some fun with you, but we won't kill you."

Slocum clicked the loaded cylinder into his six-shooter and fired in the direction of Quince's voice. He didn't have a target; he just wanted to shut the man up. The last thing Slocum wanted was for Clint Bendix to believe the outlaw would let them ride away unscathed.

"Fire, damn you, shoot!" Slocum shouted. "Fill 'em with lead. That's why you came out here." He got the others shooting wildly. Their slugs ripped through the forest and the shebang and off into thin air. That they didn't have good targets didn't matter. Slocum wanted Quince's men to duck so they had a chance to hightail it.

He rode between Bendix and the house, shooting at anything moving. Over his shoulder, Slocum said, "Get out of here. Now!"

"But my wagons! They're out back. I can see 'em!"

"You'll see them from six feet under." Slocum began firing methodically, choosing his target before shooting. He winged one outlaw, but the rest of his effort was wasted.

"Oh," Clint Bendix said, as if it had finally occurred to him that Quince had been laying in wait. The vigilantes had ridden smack into the teeth of an ambush and now the only consideration possible was escaping alive.

Slocum laid down covering fire so that Bendix and the two men with him could retreat. Then he put his head down and got his tired horse galloping after them. Lead sang all around him, but he was out of shotgun range. He reined back when he got a few hundred yards away and saw Clint Bendix all alone.

"The others head back to town already?" guessed Slocum.

Bendix nodded numbly. He looked stunned at their swift reversal of fortune. He had led the posse with high expectations, and his plan had fallen apart in a single heartbeat.

"Quince is no fool. Scouts along the road probably warned him we were coming. Or maybe someone in Orofino took word to him." Slocum held down a surge of anger, thinking that Jane might be the one who had alerted Quince. She was like a spider in the middle of a web, hearing everything that went on in town. That meant she knew Quince and might be on his payroll. A pretty woman working in a saloon would be an invaluable source of information for a swindler like Quince.

"You're right, Slocum. I never thought he'd expect us. With so many men, I thought he'd—" A bullet took off Bendix's hat and sent it flying. The man grabbed futilely, both hands resting on his balding pate.

"Get out of here. I'll keep them off your tail."

Slocum reached over and grabbed the rifle riding at Bendix's knee. He swung it around and levered a round into the chamber. When an incautious outlaw stepped out from behind a maple, Slocum drew a bead and fired. The rifle bucked hard against his shoulder but he felt good about the shot. He didn't have to see the outlaw double over and drop to his knees to know he had fired right on target.

"Go!" Slocum shouted. Bendix spurred his tired horse toward Orofino, leaving Slocum in the center of the road. He studied the wooded area where the sniper had been but saw no other outlaws coming out. This told him they were probably going to get their horses and pursue.

Slocum decided to take the fight to Quince.

Bending low, he rode through the low-hanging limbs and deeper into the forest until he came to a small clearing. Slocum got his bearings, cut sharply to his right and got ready for another fight. He came out of the woods at the rear of the livery, near the corral where Bendix's mules had been penned. All the horses he had seen the day before were gone, confirming his suspicion that Quince had taken out after his attackers.

Slocum slid his boot from the stirrup, caught his toe under the latch on the corral gate and kicked it open. For a few seconds, the mules stirred about, not sure what having a way to freedom meant. When one finally decided it could leave, the rest followed in short order. Slocum considered setting fire to the wagons, but Clint Bendix would have his scalp if he ever found out. There had to be a way to keep Quince from profiting from his theft.

Then Slocum found himself facing the gang leader and

two of his henchmen. They came from the shebang to see what the fuss was all about.

"The mules! He let the damn mules out!" cried Quince, as he went for the six-shooter slung at his hip.

Slocum took careful aim and squeezed off a shot that would have ended the thief's vile life, but the hammer fell on a dud. He quickly levered in a new round, but the delay gave Quince and his men time to dive for cover. Slocum's first shot sailed past and into the house, ricocheting off a cooking pot. He felt a momentary pang, thinking of the stew that must have been simmering there. Then he let out a rebel yell and charged.

Quince hadn't expected this and broke and ran, giving Slocum the chance to count coup on him. Swinging his rifle barrel, Slocum landed it directly on the back of the outlaw's head, sending him facedown into the ground.

"He's killin' Quince!" shouted one of the two outlaws now behind him. Slocum looked over his shoulder, swung his rifle around and fired. This round misfired, too, but the sound was loud enough to force the men to cover.

Slocum considered chambering another round and finishing off Quince but worried the lead from the last round was still lodged in the barrel. If he fired again, the rifle might blow up in his face.

Quince struggled to his feet as Slocum wheeled about and galloped past. He used the rifle as a club and smashed the stock into the road agent's face. A fountain of blood showed he had busted Quince's nose. Slocum had to be content with inflicting only this small injury, because the rest of the gang had heard the fuss and returned on the double.

Cutting away from the shebang, Slocum took cover in a small stand of alders and let his horse get its wind back. The gang assembled and listened to Quince's incoherent orders. Slocum was less interested in what Quince said than he was in counting the outlaws. He heaved a sigh of resignation.

Twelve road agents, counting Quince. The small band of vigilantes would never have stood a chance against so many armed, vicious killers.

After his horse recovered from its plunge through the woods, Slocum guided the animal back onto the main road and warily trotted past the turnoff to the shebang. The gang was occupied listening to Quince's moans of pain and his angry cursing. This confusion brought a small smile to Slocum's lips, but that was about all he could feel good about.

He headed back to Orofino, not sure what to do next.

5

"I'd be mighty careful about saying too much in any of the saloons," Slocum warned Clint Bendix. He eyed the dark-haired bartender as she went about her business, a smile on her ruby lips and a twinkle in her azure eyes. Jane hadn't appeared the least bit upset when he and Bendix had returned, but she had already heard the story of what had happened at Quince's shebang from any of a half dozen others who had ridden in the posse. Slocum couldn't puzzle her out, but until he did, caution was the best course.

"You worry way too much, Slocum," said Bendix, deep in his own thoughts. He clung to the shot glass in his hand as if he could squeeze the life out of it—and Quince. "We got to get them wagons back 'fore those swindlers sell off the contents."

"Staying alive is more important than any bucket of Pacific oysters," Slocum advised.

"It is *not*!" raged Bendix, spilling some of his whiskey onto the green felt-topped table. His face set into a mask of rage as he leaned forward until he was inches away from Slocum. "Nobody steals from me. Nobody. I ain't givin' up. You kin drift on, if you like. I'm gonna get what's mine back."

Slocum saw how determined his friend was. He found himself balancing what he might get after Bendix sold the merchandise and the freedom of simply forgetting the past month or so of his life and moving on. If it had been a matter of money versus getting involved up to his ears in a range war, Slocum would have ridden on. But Bendix was his friend and he had promised him to see the cargo through safely to Orofino.

Getting it as far as Quince's roadhouse didn't count.

"Smashing headlong into a gang as well organized as Quince's won't get your wagons back. I slowed them down by letting the mules free of the corral."

"What?" bellowed Bendix. "You set *my* mules free? It'll take a month to round them up again. Those are the meanest, most contrary animals on the face of this earth." When he realized what he was saying, Bendix settled down. "That goes fer me, don't it?"

"The wagons won't leave the shebang until Quince either catches the mules or replaces them," Slocum said. "That buys us a little time."

"What do you reckon we ought to do? He's no use." Clint Bendix glanced in the direction of Marshal Watkins. The lawman was so drunk he kept falling out of his chair at the poker table. Every time he took a tumble, the man on either side of him would pick him up and prop him against the table so they could continue fleecing him in the game.

"He's good for nothing," Slocum agreed. "And the notion we can rally the townsfolk to flush Quince out won't work, either." This time he looked past the drunken marshal to Jane. She caught his eye, smiled brightly, winked and went back to work pouring liquor for the thirsty hard rock miners.

"I tried to find Pete and the other teamsters. They done

left town." Bendix smiled ruefully. "Leastwise, I don't
have to pay 'em."

Slocum wondered if they were the smart ones. Getting
their heads blown off trying to recover the stolen cargo
looked like a fool's errand. He touched the six-shooter at
his left side and knew he was just the fool to go on that
mission.

"I sneak out and scout the place," Slocum said.
"Quince'll have lookouts posted on the road. He probably
has a few in this very saloon watching us." Try as he
might, Slocum couldn't see anyone paying them any particular attention—except Jane. Every time Slocum looked
in her direction, she was staring boldly at him.

"That sounds good to me. We need to know what we're
gettin' into out there," Bendix said. "There's only one
small detail that'll be different, though."

Slocum said nothing as he stared at his friend. Clint
Bendix grinned crookedly.

"I'll go with you."

"Your cargo, your neck in the noose," Slocum said,
finishing his whiskey. As he and Bendix left the White
Elephant, Slocum stopped in the doorway for one quick
look back. Jane blew him a goodbye kiss.

Slocum elbowed Clint Bendix in the ribs when the man
started snoring loud enough to wake the dead. Bendix
snorted, came awake and muttered, "Sorry."

"Pay attention," Slocum whispered. They had crept
within fifty feet of the shebang and had lain behind two
fallen logs for the better part of an hour, watching as the
guards paced in front of the house and moved into the
stand of maples off to one side. Before long, the sentries
would tire, sit down for a smoke or even do as Bendix
had done and grab a few minutes of sleep.

When he was sure he could get closer, Slocum would

peer into the house. He might even get the drop on Quince.

"Them guards still sittin' on my wagons?"

"Two of them," Slocum said. It surprised him that the guards weren't burrowing under the canvas to ransack the cargo for something to eat and drink.

"Didn't take them varmints long to round up the mules. You must not have scared them much or they'd be lost in the Bitterroots by now."

Slocum let the criticism of his attempt to deny Quince the use of the mules slide past and concentrated on the circuit chosen by the guards. Although it was well past midnight, the outlaws showed no sign of relaxing their vigilance. It was almost as if they were a military unit.

Or they expected somebody important to come by.

"Think they know we came out?" asked Bendix.

Slocum considered the chance that Jane had sent a message to Quince warning him, but somehow it didn't set right with him. The notion that Quince and his gang expected someone else to show up did.

"I—"

"Quiet," whispered Slocum. He heard the faint sounds of hoofbeats heading in their direction. Reaching for his six-shooter reassured him they could fight for a spell, but against so many men with rifles and shotguns, he had no expectation of a long fight. Stealth was their only ally at the moment.

A lone rider came out of the dark. Occasional flashes off a Mexican silver concha belt betrayed his presence, but otherwise Slocum couldn't see much about the man. He was medium height, well built and moved with the grace of a striking rattler, but his face remained hidden in deep shadow under the brim of his big hat.

"Evening," called a guard, coming up with his shotgun resting in the crook of his arm.

"He knows that gent," said Bendix.

Slocum motioned his friend to silence again. Three other guards moseyed over and spoke cordially to the newcomer. None of them pointed their weapons, telling Slocum they knew the man well enough to be polite. When the concha–belt-wearing cowboy dismounted, one outlaw was quick to take the reins of his horse and lead it back to the stables.

The other guards followed into the shebang, soon joined by the two on the wagons.

"We kin steal back my goods and—"

"We wouldn't get five feet. We'd have to hitch the teams and we could only drive two of the wagons," Slocum said, distracted.

"Yeah, right. Sorry, John, my mind's all jumbled up thinkin' on how Quince bamboozled me."

"Stay here," Slocum said. "Watch my back."

Before Clint Bendix could reply, Slocum slithered like a human snake across the yard to the open door. He moved so he could peer around into the main room where Quince and the others stood while the newcomer sat in a lone chair behind the table. It didn't take much time for Slocum to figure Quince was only a hired hand and this was the real gang leader.

"We got the six wagons as smooth as silk, George," said Quince, looking pleased with himself. The smile on his face faded when the seated man leaned forward and flicked his finger across Quince's taped nose.

"You're a fool, Quince," he said. "You let some drifter do that to you. And how many times have I told you the proper way to address me?"

"Sorry, Mr. Plummer," Quince said, his hand protecting his nose against another light whack. "Didn't mean nuthin' by it."

"At least you rounded up the mules so we can move the wagons right away. I've got a market for everything in this shipment, one that'll pay a damned sight better than selling to the miners in Orofino."

"You takin' the wagons to Paradise?"

"What I'm doing with the goods isn't any of your concern," Plummer snapped. "Which six of your men can drive the wagons?"

"Now?" Quince sounded surprised.

"Of course now, you fool. I didn't come riding in with drivers from any of my other shebangs, did I?"

Slocum slipped away as the men in the room started arguing among themselves who would drive the wagons in the dark. He made his way back to where Bendix lay, a sweaty hand clutching his six-gun. Slocum counted it as good luck that Bendix hadn't plugged him.

"Back to the horses," Slocum ordered. "The man who arrived is the boss and he wants six of Quince's men to drive the wagons to another camp. From the sound of it, this isn't the only shebang in the area running the forged receipt swindle."

"There're a half dozen roads running from Boise and Lewiston in this direction," Bendix said. "That son of a bitch must be makin' a fortune off the blood and sweat of honest merchants!"

"We can be aggrieved later. Right now we have to figure out where Plummer's taking the wagons."

Clint Bendix boiled over with questions, but Slocum kept his friend quiet until they reached their horses, when he explained as much as he could of what he had overheard.

"He's gonna sell my merchandise in a place called Paradise?" Bendix scratched his chin. "Don't know I ever heard of such a place, not here in Idaho."

"New towns spring up all the time," Slocum said, mounting. He heard the braying mules and creaking leather harnesses signal the departure of the freight wagons. He put his finger to his lips to keep Bendix quiet as they made their way through the dark trees and finally emerged some distance away.

"There," Bendix said, pointing. "I kin see 'em. My wagons!"

Slocum saw that the small caravan had found a pair of deep ruts through the meadow behind the stables, telling him that George Plummer had driven more than one wagon in this direction. As they rode, Slocum had to caution Bendix continually about closing the distance. They weren't going to lose the wagons. Alerting the outlaws that they were being followed was pure folly.

After more than an hour of trailing the wagons, Slocum saw a curl of smoke rising into the clear Idaho night sky. He reached over and grabbed Bendix by the arm and halted him.

"We're close to the end of the line," Slocum said.

"Paradise?"

Slocum shrugged. "This might only be a way station Plummer uses. Or it might be a camp for a hundred hungry miners. I can't tell. All I know is that the wagons are going there."

"What do we do, John?"

Slocum worried at how anxious Bendix sounded. Every minute that passed meant he was a little less likely to recover his goods. If Plummer took the stolen wagons into a full-fledged outlaw camp, they'd be faced with rescuing the merchandise from dozens of outlaws instead of the handful back at Quince's shebang.

"Circle, come at the camp from some other direction. They aren't careless and would notice two riders following the wagons into their camp."

Slocum headed east and began arcing around to approach the camp from a different path. Clint Bendix rode beside him, mumbling to himself about losing his cargo.

"Dismount," Slocum said suddenly. "Stay with the horses, and I'll scout ahead."

"No, I'm coming with you. I have the most to lose."

"You'll lose your head if you don't keep quiet. The camp's not fifty yards ahead."

"How can you tell? Never mind. I'll keep the horses company."

Slocum moved like a silent shadow through the stand of alders until he reached the edge of a large clearing. The grass had been trampled down or eaten by the dozens of horses milling about. He tried to figure out how many men camped here and gave up trying. There might be as many as fifty in the bivouac and every last man was armed to the teeth.

The arrival of the wagons produced a ripple through the camp and loud protests Slocum couldn't quite make out. What he did see told him Plummer didn't rule the gang with an iron hand. Two men, not twenty feet off from his hiding place, argued loudly, and finally one called the other out.

"You ain't never gettin' a cut of this loot," said the smaller of the two. He widened his stance and squared off, facing the other.

The two outlaws went for their six-shooters at the same time, but the smaller one was as quick as chain lightning. He cleared leather, fired and had his six-gun back in the holster before the other man knew he was dead.

The gunfire brought others in the camp running. It also brought disaster down on Slocum's head. Crashing through the woods behind him came Clint Bendix, waving his gun around wildly.

"You all right, John? Them sons-of-bitches didn't hurt you, did they?"

The commotion in the camp died at the unexpected outcry. Then the small gunfighter threw down again and fired straight at Clint Bendix.

6

For Slocum the world moved as if dipped in molasses.
He saw the small gunfighter fire a second shot. Clouds of
white smoke drifted away from the gun muzzle in lazy
spirals. From behind him, Slocum heard Clint Bendix
gasp and then cry out in pain.

Slocum's hand flew to his Colt Navy when the spell
broke suddenly. He fired twice at the gunman and saw
the man's head snap back before he flopped onto the
ground like a fish out of water. The commotion in the
outlaw camp rose to a din, but Slocum was already back-
tracking. He heard the outlaws shouting, demanding to
know what was happening, who had shot their partner.
He paid no attention to them as he knelt beside his fallen
friend.

"John, he got me. Right through the heart. I'm dyin'."
Clint Bendix clutched his chest.

"Your heart's on the other side," Slocum said, seeing
that the bullet had hit Bendix on the right side. From the
blood seeping onto the merchant's shirt, Slocum guessed
the bullet had hit a rib and had probably broken it. But
as bad as the wound looked, it wasn't going to kill him.
Not right away.

The road agents, shouting even louder now that they were back in their camp, would, though.

Slocum got his arm around Bendix and heaved the man up and over his shoulder, carrying him like a sack of potatoes.

"Why'd you come running like that?" Slocum asked as he made his way through the dark toward their horses. He didn't hear any pursuit behind, but knew it was only a matter of time before somebody figured out the gunfighter had been shot by a sniper outside their camp.

"The shootin'," Bendix said weakly. "I thought they'd done you in. Couldn't let 'em get by doin' that, not to you, not to a friend . . ." Bendix passed out from pain as Slocum jolted him along. It took the better part of ten minutes for Slocum to get Bendix heaved up and over his saddle.

Another five minutes passed while he tied the man down so he wouldn't slide off.

Then, as if he walked on eggshells, Slocum led both horses away from the camp. Every sense alert for pursuit, he put almost a mile between himself and the road agents before he mounted and set a quicker pace. For some reason, the outlaws didn't chase after him. Slocum wondered if any of the cutthroats cared that the gunfighter had been shot. They might be accusing each other—or congratulating one another.

Dawn thrust pink and orange fingers into the sky by the time Slocum reached Orofino. He hadn't bothered checking Bendix to see if the man was dead or alive. If he could survive, he was tough enough to do it. If he had died, there wasn't anything more Slocum could have done for him. But Slocum still worried about tending the man. If the best the larger town of Lewiston had was a vet, there wouldn't be a doctor at all in Orofino.

As he rode down the street, eyes searching for a barber

or anybody else likely to have some medical knowledge, he heard a cheery voice calling to him.

"Hello! John! How are you?"

He twisted in the saddle and saw Jane coming out of the White Elephant. She had a shawl around her shoulders and appeared as sassy as she had when they'd first met.

"Good morning," Slocum said in greeting, touching the brim of his hat politely. "You're up early."

"Late," Jane said. "Just got off work." She came over and saw Bendix slung over the saddle. "What happened, John? He's been shot!"

"Is there a sawbones in town?" he asked.

"Don't know of one this side of Boise," she said. "There's not even a decent vet in these parts, though the farrier doubles, sometimes, but only with horses. The town butcher might patch up a gunshot, if it's not too bad."

Slocum laughed harshly. Turning Bendix over to a hog butcher would certainly mean death.

"I . . . I might be of some help. I've patched up some gunshot wounds. Not many, but some." Jane bit her lip and looked stricken at the idea of dealing with a man likely to up and die because of what she did.

"I've got a little experience, too," Slocum said. During the war he had seen so-called doctors amputate arms and legs in seconds. Few of their patients survived, but some had and Slocum had picked up a few pointers on tending their wounds. Clint Bendix wasn't that bad off, but if the rib had punctured a lung, the man's death warrant had been signed. Eventually, he would drown in his own blood.

"Come on over to my place. I've got a shack on the outskirts of town." She looked up at him. Slocum thought she looked even more beautiful now, worried and showing great concern for Bendix, than she did when she was flirt-

ing with him—and every other man in the White Elephant
Saloon.

"It'll be messy," Slocum warned.

Jane already hiked along with great determination for
the far side of town. Slocum rose slowly behind, enjoying
the sight of her rear end swishing this way and that as
she hurried along. They got a quarter mile from the edge
of Orofino before she turned to a ramshackle house that
had more holes than boards in its walls.

"It's not much, but it's the best I could do."

"Boomtown," Slocum said, a little surprised, as he
wrestled Bendix inside, that evidence pointed to Jane living alone. A lovely woman like her had to have men buzz-
ing around like bees to a fresh new blossom. He dropped
Bendix onto the bed and got a moan in return.

"He's still alive," Jane said, blinking at the sight of his
entire shirt being blood-soaked.

Slocum drew his thick-bladed knife and began cutting
away the cloth and peeling off the parts dried into the
wound. As grisly as it looked, Slocum saw that the wound
wasn't anywhere near as bad as he had expected.

"I'll boil some water. We have to clean that right away
before infection sets in."

Slocum ripped up what remained of Bendix's shirt to
use as a bandage when they reached that point. The hot
water soaked off the clot and let Slocum probe gently for
bone fragments. He found two small pieces and teased
them out with the point of his knife.

"I'm glad you're doing that, John," Jane said. "I
wouldn't be any good. My hands would shake. They *are*
shaking." She held them out to show him.

"When did you clean a bullet wound before?" he asked.

"I've drifted around the past year or so and have seen
about everything. Or I thought so," she said.

"Miss Jane, if you can hold this end of the bandage in
place, I'll tie it off."

"Miss Jane?" This brought a real laugh to her lips. "Jane is fine. The name's Jane Garson. I didn't bother giving you the full moniker before."

"I understand," Slocum said. "A woman working in a saloon can't get too friendly or a man'd misunderstand."

"I do just fine with the miners. They've staked out their claims and I've done the same. By now they know when they're trespassing."

"On another man's claim?" Slocum asked.

"Here, John. Let me tie that." She showed more dexterity than he expected as she cinched down the crude bandage on Bendix's chest. Jane stepped back, hands bloody, and watched him for a few seconds. "He's resting easy now. No sign of uneven breathing and his pulse is strong."

"You have the knack to be a nurse," Slocum said.

"Not me, never. I don't like getting all bloody." She held up her hands and looked at them. "I need to clean off. Why don't you leave him and come along to the stream? You can do with a bit of sprucing up, too."

"Reckon he'll be all right. We've done what we can for him." Slocum saw that Jane fumbled around and got out a large towel from a grip at the foot of the bed. He hadn't considered where she kept her clothes and personal belongings until now. This, as much as anything else, showed she was a transient like all the others in Orofino. Somehow, this bit of information pleased Slocum.

"Sun's warming up the forest by now," she said, looking east. The birds chirped and the wind had died down so the only scent coming to Slocum was from the fragrant spruce and fir trees nearby. "The stream's over yonder."

She set off, Slocum trailing again and not minding. Jane found a well-trod path that led directly to the shore of a stream a few yards wide. It looked as if it might be waist-deep in the middle, but the swift current would make standing difficult.

Slocum turned from the stream and looked around. His hand flashed to his six-shooter.

"Jane! Where are you?"

"Over here, John," she said. A delighted laugh followed her words.

He didn't holster his pistol until he rounded a large boulder and found a shallow pool. His eyes widened and his heart began beating faster when he saw her.

"I have my own personal bathtub." She turned toward him and stood from the shallow pool. Jane had shucked off her clothes and was buck naked. Gloriously naked.

"Why don't I join you?"

Her broad grin was all the invitation he needed. Slocum stripped off his boots and gun belt, took off his shirt and had begun wiggling from his jeans when Jane came over.

"My, my, no wonder you're having such a hard time getting those pants off. You're so . . . long." She reached out and wrapped her cool, wet fingers around his erection. Gently stroking, she got him harder than a steel bar before she dropped to her knees in the water and bent her head down to his groin.

A thrill passed through Slocum as her lips touched his organ. He sat down heavily, feet in the water as he propped himself up on his elbows. Looking down he saw the top of Jane's head moving up and down slowly. He heard the lewd sucking sounds she made, but the feel throughout his loins counted most. Every time her tongue touched him, it was as if a Fourth of July skyrocket went off. Her teeth raked the delicate underside and sent alternating hot and cold jabs of pure delight into his loins. But most of all he relished the feel of her lips moving up and down along his rigid length.

Reaching down, he laced his fingers through her lustrous dark hair and guided her head in a motion that drove him wild. He thrust upward into her mouth and then sank back when she retreated. Her tongue began dancing around, turning him even weaker.

"My, you're so big," she said, looking up. A broad grin split her face. She licked her lips sensuously and then said, "I'd like to find out how big."

"Can't you tell? Do you think your eyes are deceiving you?" he asked, knowing what she suggested but wanting to tease her a mite.

"I can tell if my eyes are bigger than my appetite, using the right techniques." Jane pushed away from him and flopped in the shallow pool, kicking up spray in his direction. Sitting in the middle of the pond, she lifted her knees so they poked up out of the water. She braced herself on her hands and leaned back so the gentle waves in the pond lapped up across her belly.

A ray of morning sun slanted through the trees and caressed her snowy white breasts. The tips were capped with rock-hard nubs and the sleek cones showed gooseflesh from the cold water. Slocum couldn't let such tasty looking morsels go unsampled.

He entered the cold pool of water and felt himself melting as water surged around him. But only for a moment. His excitement mounted anew as he licked and sucked and savored the twin delights Jane presented for his enjoyment.

He raked his tongue up one side and down into the deep valley between her teats, then worked his way up the other until he caught the rubbery nip between his lips. It was her turn to moan and thrash about as he applied suction to her tender flesh.

When Jane fell back into the water and her legs rose on either side of his body, he knew it was time to quit playing and start giving them both the real pleasure they sought. He cupped her breasts in his hands as he slid closer into the vee of her sleek thighs. His manhood had turned into iron again after the sudden dousing in the cold water.

"Oh, yes, yes!" she gasped out as he entered her, proving he was even stiffer than when she had mouthed him.

Slocum bent forward and levered his hips forward powerfully. He sank balls-deep into her seething hot interior. For a moment, he paused, reveling in the clutching female sheath, then he pulled back with deliberate slowness. Every inch of his retreat sent new electric tingles throughout both their bodies. Slocum looked down and saw that Jane had her eyes closed. Her hair floated on the pond and tiny droplets of water dotted her marvelous breasts.

The sight of her body and the sounds of her ecstasy built the pressures within him. He thrust forward again, sloshing water around. The feel against his naked body, across hers, caused the tides of passion to rise. He began stroking with firm, powerful strokes. This drove Jane wild with desire. She half sat up, her fingers clawing at his upper arms and back. He felt her nails raking his skin but ignored it.

He moved even faster, thrusting forward and back until the heat of friction burned his senses. Jane gasped and writhed under him, splashing water everywhere. Slocum sped up until he was moving like a railroad engine's piston. Deeper, harder—then Jane cried out in release.

Her entire body quivered beneath him, around him. Her strong inner muscles crashed down around his buried length and Slocum let his load fly. He spewed furiously until he was entirely spent, then sank on top of her.

Their faces only inches apart, he closed the distance and lightly kissed her. Then he rolled to one side in the pond and let the water wash over his naked body.

"My, my," Jane said dreamily. "That's not the way I remembered it."

"What?"

"It was better!" Jane rolled onto her side in the water

and put her arm around him. She scooted closer and kissed him, then let her hands go exploring on his muscular body.

"A pretty woman like you . . . ," he began.

"Can have any man she wants," Jane said. She kissed him hard, with obvious need. "And I want you, John Slocum. Again!"

They scared the fish in the stream and neither of them cared.

7

"I don't know if he's going to get much better," Jane said, looking at Clint Bendix. The merchant lay on his back, mouth open and sucking in air noisily.

"It's only been a couple days," Slocum said, but he knew what she meant. He was getting itchy feet doing nothing but tending to Bendix. Jane had gone to work and returned a couple times, her schedule unchanged by the presence of two guests. Unchanged, that is, except by the pleasurable way she and Slocum had spent the nights while Bendix snored away. As good as it had been, Slocum felt as if he had to be doing something other than acting as nurse.

"I can't do anything for him if you ride off, John," Jane said. "The boss'd fire me in a flash if I didn't show up at the White Elephant. The only reason most of those miners come into the place to get drunk is me. There're a dozen other places with cheaper booze."

"That means he'd be a fool to fire you."

"You don't know Chauncey. He's mean as a wharf rat. The first night I worked there he watched me like I intended to steal him blind. He trusts me now. A little."

Jane laughed her musical laugh and added, "A very little, though."

"You could get a job at any other place in Orofino," Slocum pointed out. He felt the pressure of time heavily. By now George Plummer had moved the six wagons to wherever he had intended selling the contents and probably had hijacked another shipment or two using the forged receipt swindle. If Slocum couldn't get Bendix's goods back, he could squeeze a considerable amount of gold coin out of the outlaw leader and then put a stop to his predation.

"Chauncey would bust the saloon up the minute I stepped behind the bar. He's *mean,* John, mad-dog, rabid-weasel, stepped-on-rattler mean."

"You don't intend working for him forever, do you?"

"No, but when I find what I'm looking for, I can move on and he won't dare follow." Jane looked pensive.

"What are you looking for?"

Before she could answer, Bendix stirred and rolled onto his side. His eyes blinked open and he spoke.

"Surely am powerful hungry. You got anything to feed a dyin' man?"

"You're not dying," Slocum said. "In fact, Jane and I were discussing if you were up to a little ride."

"Where'd that be? To the potter's field?"

Slocum snorted and shook his head in amazement.

"You're going to outlive the lot of us. From what I've heard about Marshal Watkins, he'll be worse than worthless tracking down the swindlers who stole your goods."

"Plummer," grumbled Bendix. "I'll never forget that son of a bitch's name."

"Plummer?" asked Jane, frowning. "I remember hearing some of the miners talking about a man named Plummer. He is one mean hombre, from the way they turn all pale when they even say his name."

"Might be you should put him and Chauncey in the

same room and let them savage each other," Slocum said. He got his arm around Bendix and helped him sit up.

"I'm a bit dizzy but suppose I'm up to ridin' outta here," Clint Bendix said. "If Watkins is as worthless as tits on a bull, then we got to get back to Lewiston. Sheriff Allen might be the most honest lawman in these parts."

"Allen? Never heard of him," Jane said, "but then they go through marshals and sheriffs mighty fast around here."

"I can ride, Slocum," Bendix insisted. "Since I don't hear mules brayin' outside or see mountains of crates with my merchandise, that means you been sittin' on your butt and doin' nothin'."

"Why, John's been like a doctor to you. He—"

"Enough, Jane," Slocum said. "He's pulling my leg. Bendix knows he would have died if I hadn't brought him here."

"Slocum doctorin' me? It's amazin' I'm still alive, then. No, 'less I miss a guess, it's because a heavenly angel named Jane has been by my bedside nursin' me back to health."

"Are you Irish?" Jane asked. "I've never heard such blarney!"

"If bein' Irish would keep you tendin' me, why I was born in the County Kerry and—"

"I'll saddle the horses before I get too disgusted," Slocum said. Jane gave him one of her magnificent smiles as he left. He didn't doubt for an instant that Bendix knew what had been going on between them while he recovered. It was his way of funning with them.

Slocum got the saddles on, Bendix's still caked with the man's blood. There wasn't any way Slocum could get the bloodstains off and he didn't try. He led the horses around to the front of the shack as Jane helped Bendix out. Slocum was glad to see that, in spite of how much the merchant leaned on the woman, Bendix mostly walked on his own.

"If you're done copping a feel, let me help you up," Slocum said.

"I can do it myself, thank you kindly." Clint Bendix turned, bowed and kissed Jane's hand. "Be back soon, little angel." Then he put an unsteady foot in the stirrup and dragged himself up.

"Will you be back?" Jane asked. It might have been in response to Bendix, but Slocum knew the question was directed at him. He nodded briskly, tipped his hat and then headed his pony back in the direction of Lewiston with Bendix right behind.

"You're not gonna die in my office, are you?" Sheriff Allen looked hard at Clint Bendix.

"Hell, I won't even bleed on your floor, Sheriff," Bendix said. He dropped into a straight-backed chair. It creaked under his bulk and tilted a little but didn't dump him onto the floor. Bendix steadied himself by grabbing the edge of the lawman's desk.

"Who shot you up?" Sheriff Allen asked the question of Bendix but stared at Slocum.

"A man by the name of George Plummer. At least, it was someone in his gang."

"Plummer? Don't know the name." Allen rummaged through a two-inch-thick stack of wanted posters and dropped them where Slocum could leaf through them. Slocum hesitated, wondering if one bearing his likeness was in the pile.

While Slocum studied the posters one by one, Clint Bendix told the sheriff all that had happened at Quince's shebang and how they had followed the stolen wagons to the camp. Slocum finally came across a poster bearing Plummer's ugly face.

"That the gent?" Allen took the poster and stuck it to

the wall with a wad of tobacco juice so anyone coming into the office could see it. "There. He's got a decent enough reward on his head."

"Five hundred dollars," Bendix said, "is hardly enough to pay me back for what he stole. Him and that yahoo Quince."

"Tell you what," Allen said. "I got me two new deputies who can look after matters here in Lewiston for a day or two. What do you say we ride back to Orofino and see if I can't build a fire under that no-good Watkins."

"You're not his boss," Slocum said.

"Don't you think I look mean enough to make him do his job? If I don't, maybe I can scare him out of the territory so Orofino can hire a marshal who'll do his duty."

"What do you expect Marshal Watkins to do?" asked Slocum.

"I need a few men riding at my back 'fore I take on Plummer and Quince. I'll start low and work up, but I can't arrest Quince with just you and Bendix beside me, not if what you say is true about them having an army of outlaws at their beck and call."

"Count Bendix out," Slocum said. "He's still too weak."

"Wait, Slocum, you can't deal me out of this hand. It's my merchandise they stole."

"Rest up. The sheriff and I'll take care of them."

"Sounds like Mr. Slocum's givin' you some sage advice. I'd take it."

Slocum said nothing more, letting Bendix come to his own conclusion. Sheriff Allen struck him as a diligent lawman. Under other circumstances, that might be a problem but now Slocum was on the side of the law.

"All right, but don't you go get yourself kilt, Slocum. I won't talk to you again if you do."

Slocum laughed and said, "That's a promise."

• • •

"Don't look like your Miss Garson is anywhere to be seen," Allen said, climbing back into the saddle.

Slocum looked around the shack and decided Jane had gone on into Orofino to work.

"She'll be at the White Elephant," he said.

"Heard tell of it. Quite a reputation, and not a good one," Allen said. He sat a little stiffer in the saddle and looked as if he had bitten into a sour persimmon.

"You a teetotaler, Sheriff?" asked Slocum, taking a stab in the dark at what drove the man.

"Yes, sir, I am. My wife's strongly in favor of prohibition and I go along with her. Our entire church congregation does, in fact."

Slocum said nothing more as they rode into Orofino. As he reined back in front of the White Elephant Saloon a scrawny man with a massive handlebar mustache came boiling out.

"Took you long enough to get here," the man shouted. "They done took her. Waltzed right on in, stuck a gun in my belly and took her."

"Who might that be?" asked the sheriff, but Slocum had a cold feeling he knew what the man meant.

"My barkeep, Jane Garson. They kidnapped her!"

"You're Chauncey?" asked Slocum. "The owner?"

"Who else would give two hoots in hell about a slut like her?" Chauncey wilted a little under Slocum's cold gaze. "Well, it's true. Nobody looks after their help like I do."

"How long?" asked Slocum.

"Not more'n twenty minutes. A half hour. They marched her down the street, to the north. Don't know what they wanted with her, but they threatened me."

Slocum tugged on his reins and got his horse into a trot but suddenly drew rein when he passed another saloon. From inside came raucous laughter and off-key singing.

Mingled with it was Jane's urging to drink more.

"She's inside," Slocum said.

"Are you sure, Slocum?"

Slocum hit the ground and went to the doorway. It had been squared better than the one leading into the White Elephant and had a door on hinges, but inside there seemed to be no difference. Jane stood behind the bar pouring liquor as fast as she could. Three men in front of her knocked back the whiskey and produced all the noise Slocum had heard from outside.

Jane put her finger to her lips, cautioning Slocum to silence.

"You boys deserve another drink. On the house. You've been on the trail so long, it's not going to hurt if you wet your whistle just a little more."

"S'long's yer buyin'," the tallest of the trio said. As he drank the whiskey, his legs turned wobbly and he sank to the floor, passed out on the way down.

"Lookee there, ole Clint cain't hold his likker," said the man next to him. Then he collapsed. The third man stood like rock, not moving until Slocum went to him and gently shoved. Like a tree felled by a lumberjack, the man crashed to the floor.

"What's going on?" demanded Sheriff Allen.

"These four decided to kidnap me, but I talked them into stopping for a drink." Jane reached under the bar and put a small bottle filled with clear liquid on top of it. "What every bar has. Knockout drops."

"You gave them a Mickey Finn?" Slocum found himself laughing.

"After they decided they wanted to do a little drinking, it was easy enough."

"They kidnapped you? You want to prefer charges?"

"I suppose," Jane said, looking at Slocum. "Do you know them?"

Slocum looked at the three and scratched his head.

"Never seen them before, but then Quince had a small army with him and Plummer had even more."

"You reckon they work for those two?"

"They knew I'd helped Clint Bendix," Jane said.

"Don't much matter what their reason was. They did the crime, they do the time."

"You said four of them came for you," Slocum said. "Where's the last one?"

Jane laughed, stepped to one side and pointed to the floor behind the bar. Slocum leaned over and saw the fourth kidnapper stretched out with a big lump on his head.

"I got him with a bung starter. The other three never noticed."

"Dumb as dirt, the lot of them," Allen said, grunting as he dragged a pair out of the saloon by their collars. He came back for the other two.

"I need to have words with the marshal. These sidewinders are all his, since you can't rightly say they were involved in stealing Mr. Bendix's goods. They committed their crime within the town limits of Orofino, making it the local law's concern."

"I'll watch over them until you fetch the marshal," Slocum said.

"From what you've told me, it might be a spell. I might have to sober the marshal up with a few cups of coffee."

As Sheriff Allen left, Jane asked in her light tone, "Buy you a drink, John?"

8

"Chauncey is a real Simon Legree," Jane said, coming around the bar in the White Elephant Saloon. She wiped her hands on the filthy apron, then took it off, tossed it on the end of the bar and held out her arm for Slocum to take.

He escorted her into the early morning. Chauncey had insisted that she work until she made up the time she had been away from the saloon. It didn't matter to him that she had been forcibly taken from the White Elephant— he wanted his money's worth out of her. And Slocum was intrigued that she gave it to him.

"He's a slave driver," Slocum agreed, "but why do you stay here?"

"I have my reasons, John," she said as they walked along the deserted street. This might be the only time of day that Orofino was silent. Miners drank and caroused far into the night and the merchants didn't open their stores until sunrise. This predawn period was when the miners passed out before they started another day of back-breaking work in their gold pits. No one hurrahed the town, no freight wagons moved—it was as silent as a grave.

Slocum found himself liking it, all the more so because Jane was on his arm.

"They have to be good ones. You could go to a bigger town and make twice what you are here."

"And not have to cope with Chauncey and his vile ways," she finished.

For several minutes she walked along without speaking; then she said, "I'm looking for someone."

Slocum felt her tense and knew she had to spit it out on her own. It wouldn't speed the recitation up one iota if he broke the train of her thought by asking questions she wanted to sidestep.

"I'm looking for someone important, and you might help, John. Will you?"

"Depends," he said cautiously. He thought the world of Jane Garson but wasn't going to dive into any muddy water without knowing what lay beneath the surface.

"Ever the discreet man," she said, smiling. "I'll tell you everything and not ask you if you'll help. You can tell me if you will. If you can."

Jane took a deep breath. Slocum watched her breasts rise and fall under her beer-sodden blouse and tried not to be too distracted by the way her nipples were outlined perfectly against the damp cloth.

"It's my husband. I'm hunting for him."

Slocum felt as if he had been punched in the belly.

"You're married?" he got out.

"I'm not sure. Oh, I know how that sounds, but George lit out and I haven't seen him in almost a year. I've heard tell that he's dead. If he is, I want to find the body and give him a proper burial."

"If he's alive?"

Jane shrugged. "He's a low-down, no-account snake for leaving me the way he did. I waited for him one Saturday, had dinner prepared and he never showed up. And I had fixed his favorite, peach cobbler, too."

This latter seemed to cause her more distress than anything else. Slocum held his tongue, waiting for the rest of the story.

"I spent all that Sunday asking after him, and one of his friends named Luke Latham claimed he had ridden out, but there were rumors that Luke had gunned him down and hid the body."

"What did the marshal say?"

Jane laughed harshly. "The marshal where we came from over in Nebraska was even more a drunk than Watkins. Worse, he was as crooked as a dog's hind leg. He told me he would track down George—for a price."

"He wasn't talking about money, was he?"

"I kicked him in the balls as hard as I could," she said hotly. Then Jane's mood changed mercurially. "I had to clear out of town pretty quick after that."

"I've followed Latham ever since, always a few days behind him. But he's somewhere around Orofino and has been for a month."

"Ever since you showed up," Slocum said.

"He beat me here by a bit. It took me months to track him, but he's here. I've asked about him and more than one miner's seen Latham. Or thinks he has. It's hard for me to take time to go track down the sightings, so I wait at the White Elephant figuring Latham'll come in sooner or later."

"Any word about your husband?"

"Not a peep. George Garson always played his cards close to the vest. If he got tired of me, he's not likely to go shooting off his mouth about what he left behind."

"How'd any man get tired of you?" asked Slocum.

"Oh, John, you're so sweet." Jane giggled like a schoolgirl. "I'll bet you don't hear that too often." She ran her fingers over his powerful biceps and across the broad chest rippling with muscles. Slocum was tall, lank, and made of whipcord and pure mean.

"I don't," Slocum allowed. "If I go looking for your husband, what do I do when I find him?"

"Dead, I want to see his grave. And if he's alive," Jane said, her jaw set, "I might just put him in that grave. No, that's not true. I *have* thought of it. I had a sheaf of divorce papers all drawn up. I'll make the louse sign them."

This wasn't what Slocum had expected.

"If he upped and left you, why not ignore him the way he is you?"

"Remarry, you mean, without a proper divorce—or death? I couldn't do that. It just wouldn't be right. Sorry, John, but it's my upbringing. Life has to have some order, and I'm not the one who makes the rules."

Slocum disagreed about breaking laws but saw how determined Jane was on this point.

"Tell me about Luke Latham. If he's nosing around, having a talk with him is the only way I can see to find what's happened to your husband."

"A real lowlife," Jane said, "but he and George were always thicker than thieves."

"Describe him," Slocum said, listening as Jane went into detail about Latham's appearance. As she rambled on, Slocum got the feeling he had seen Luke Latham recently but couldn't put his finger on it.

"It's sunrise," Jane said suddenly, coming to a halt in front of the door of her tumbledown shack.

"I'd better get on Latham's trail," Slocum said.

"After the sun gets up a little. After *this* gets up a little more," she said, moving closer and running her hand down his taut belly and then skipping over his crotch. Slocum wanted to argue but didn't.

Slocum looked up from the poker hand. In another game he would have bet the sky and earth and then hunted for something else to throw into the pot. The number of times he had ever seen four aces in his hand could be counted on a couple fingers. But he hesitated to bet. This was a penny-ante game, and he wanted something more than the pot.

He was on the brink of getting real information.

"Luke Latham, yeah, the name's familiar," the miner said. "Real bastard, if you ask me. He's a sneak thief workin' for George Plummer. You heard of him?"

"The fellow who runs the shebangs?" Slocum asked. He stared at his hand and felt like a racehorse at the starting line. He wanted to push to the limit but knew he couldn't or he'd scare off the miner.

"That's him. A swindler if ever there was one." The miner held his cards close to his chest, and Slocum knew the man thought he was a winner.

"Where can I find Latham?" Slocum read the answer on the man's face. If he won, he'd feel more accommodating.

"What're you gonna do?"

"Fold," Slocum said with a heavy heart, throwing in the four aces.

"Yipeee!" the miner crowed. "First big pot I got in more'n a month." He raked in his winnings. Slocum was glad he didn't see the hand. From the way the man's tells played out, he didn't have more than two pair.

"Where can I find him?" asked Slocum.

"Behind you. At the bar, drinkin' like there was no tomorrow. Buy you a drink, mister?"

Slocum swung around. He scanned the faces of the men intent on getting drunk, then stopped when he got to the man at the middle of the bar. His hand moved involuntarily to the butt of his six-shooter.

"Reckon not. See you around." The miner had noticed how Slocum reacted to finding Luke Latham and didn't want to push his luck by getting between two men intent on gunning down each other.

Slocum thought he had recognized Latham from Jane's

description. Seeing Luke Latham in the flesh told him why. This was the owlhoot back in Lewiston who had been nosing around Bendix's wagons and taking inventory so Quince could draw up the fake receipt.

He left the poker table, drew his Colt Navy and stood directly behind Latham. As Slocum leaned over, as if to get another drink from the barkeep, he shoved the barrel into Latham's back.

"Move and I'll ventilate you," Slocum said. "We're going to leave—out the back way to the alley."

"Mister, I ain't got any money. I spent it all on booze."

"Shut up and move."

"Don't kill me, mister. I got a wife and kids. They—"

"Shut up," Slocum repeated, using the six-gun to steer the outlaw outside. In the alley, he shoved Latham against the saloon wall. "Keep your hands where I can see them."

"I told you," Latham whined. "I'm busted, broke, no money. Check my pockets. You'll see."

"I'm not trying to rob you. I want information."

"I don't know nuthin'."

Slocum cocked his six-shooter and held it a few inches from Latham's face. The man began to sweat like a pig.

"I'll tell you what I know for a fact," Slocum said. "You work for George Plummer and you helped him and Quince steal my friend's cargo. I saw you making the inventory back in Lewiston. In fact, I chased you off when I should have put a bullet in your black heart."

"Please, mister, I don't know what you're talkin' about."

Slocum ignored the outburst. He knew feigned innocence when he heard it. He was positive Latham was in cahoots with Quince.

"I'm willing to let you ride out of Orofino in exchange for some information."

"Anything. Don't kill me."

"George Garson. Where can I find him?"

"Garson? You're joking, right? What do you want with him?"

"It's personal. Where is he? Is he still alive?"

Luke Latham licked dried lips and his eyes darted about like a trapped rat's. He would lie rather than tell the truth but if he could escape, he'd go that route. Slocum shoved him hard back against the wall and pressed the cold muzzle of his Colt against the man's forehead.

"Talk," Slocum said.

Latham's mouth opened and then snapped shut. Something changed in his eyes, and Slocum wondered what caused it.

Then he heard the double hammers on a shotgun cocking behind him.

"Don't want to make a mess of you, mister, but I'll do it 'less you put down that hogleg."

Slocum glanced over his shoulder and saw the feckless Orofino marshal.

"I got a thief," Slocum said.

"Wrong. *I* got a thief. You. If you don't hand over that six-shooter, I'll fill you with double-ought buckshot!"

Slocum stepped back from Latham, letting the man bolt like a frightened rabbit. He watched the swindler vanish around the side of the saloon and knew he'd have to track him down again.

"Let's mosey on over to the jail, mister. Me and you got some serious talkin' over to do about how the law's enforced in my town."

Marshal Watkins herded Slocum to the rickety town calaboose and put him in the solitary cell. The sound of the lock clicking shut was like a peal of doom for Slocum.

9

Slocum scratched as the fleas began chewing on his hide. He sat up on the straw pallet thrown on the floor of the jail cell and looked over to the marshal's desk. The keys were almost within reach. Almost. Slocum had been in some secure jails and some that were more like a sieve. This was the first one that almost begged him to break out.

That was why he hesitated. It was too easy.

He stood and scratched some more, then put his hands on the bars. They had rusted through. A good jerk would pull them out of their bases or even break the bars into pieces. If he didn't feel inclined to exert himself that much, Slocum knew he could kick open the door if he didn't mind raising a ruckus. The lock was a joke.

And then there were the keys tantalizing inches from his grip on the desk. Slocum sat back down on the straw pallet and listened hard.

In the street out front of the jail he heard two men arguing. He recognized Marshal Watkins's voice right away and thought the other might be Luke Latham's. The gist of what he overheard was how tired they were getting waiting for Slocum to make a break for freedom.

He smiled wryly, knowing he had outwitted them. They expected him to break out and walk into a couple leveled six-shooters. Before he hit the dirt of Orofino's main street, they'd have him in a wagon bound for the cemetery on the outskirts of town. That would end their dilemma about what to do with him legally.

Slocum's smile faded when he remembered that Watkins wasn't any high-level thinker. When Slocum didn't fall into his clumsy trap, he would simply walk in and shoot his prisoner in the cell. That lacked finesse or legal endorsement but who would care? Slocum was a drifter in a boomtown filled with transients. The closest anyone came to being a permanent resident might be Marshal Watkins.

The outer door opened. For a brief instant Slocum caught sight of Latham. The man jerked around and hurried off to keep from being identified. Everything Slocum had learned about the man showed he was inept and as dim-witted as Watkins. They made quite a pair. Slocum wondered if either had bothered telling their real boss about their prisoner.

If not, Slocum still had a chance to capture Plummer and Quince. But that would have to be postponed until he got free of the town lockup and beat the information about Jane's husband out of Luke Latham.

"How much is bail, Marshal?" asked Slocum.

"More'n you got, cowboy. It's a serious matter pullin' a gun on a law-abidin' citizen of my town."

"Where does Latham hang his hat? Somewhere nearby?"

"You don't ask no questions. That's my prerogative." The marshal smiled, proud of knowing such legal words.

Slocum lounged back and stared at the marshal until Watkins turned a little edgy.

"What you starin' at me for, boy?"

"I was wondering what it costs to buy a marshal. A real

one might go for a sizable pile of gold, but you? Ten dollars? That much?"

"You shut yer tater trap," shouted Watkins, angrily coming to the cell. "I ain't bought and sold by no one."

"Not even Plummer?" Slocum saw the shot had hit the bull's-eye. Watkins turned red in the face as he gripped the bars from outside the cell. For a moment, Slocum thought the marshal was going to rip down the bars in his rage. The outer door opened and caused Watkins to whirl around.

"What you want?" he demanded. His manner didn't soften much when he saw Jane Garson.

"Good afternoon, Marshal," she said politely. Jane clutched a small purse and looked like some prim, proper schoolmarm. Slocum knew that wasn't the way she was at all, not in private.

"Get out of my jailhouse," Watkins said. "No visitors allowed."

"I've come to post bail for Mr. Slocum. I heard of his misfortune and wanted to do something to thank him for rescuing me from those awful kidnappers." Jane craned her neck and looked past the marshal into the cell. "Where *are* the men who kidnapped me? I thought Sheriff Allen told you to keep them locked up until trial."

"There wasn't enough evidence to hold them. I had to let 'em go."

"What! Why, I had not even given you a statement. How could you say there wasn't any evidence when you didn't ask for any?"

"No bail," Watkins grumbled. "Too serious a crime."

"Disorderly conduct is a worse felony than kidnapping? Why, Marshal Watkins, if I didn't know better I'd think you were harboring a grudge against Mr. Slocum."

"I do my job," Watkins said. He looked around frantically, as if Latham might come to his rescue. Or Plummer. Jane obviously had him on the run with her questioning.

"Then set bail so I can get Mr. Slocum out. He has chores to do for me."

"He's workin' for you?"

"Something like that," Jane said. She ignored Slocum shaking his head vigorously, trying to warn her away from such an admission.

"No bail, not till the circuit judge comes along to set the bail. That might not be for another month or two. Heard tell Judge Callabasian don't hold much to schedules."

"I'm sure I wouldn't know. I'm equally sure you don't, either," Jane said. Slocum finally caught her eye and waved her off. "I suppose I should hire a lawyer to plead Mr. Slocum's case."

"Ain't none in Orofino. Leastwise, none that don't have a couple bullets in their heart or necks stretched from a hangman's noose. Lawyers complicate life too much to be tolerated in a town like this."

Jane harrumphed and left without another word. Slocum waited for Watkins to draw his six-gun and put a slug in him, but another ruckus outside drew the marshal's attention.

He had barely opened the office door when a miner came flying in, hit flat on his belly and slid until his head crashed into the bars of the cell.

"I want him locked up till he's sober," growled Chauncey. "I won't have no drunk miner bustin' up my place."

"There's no room," Watkins said, his hand on the butt of his pistol. He was itching to shoot Slocum but something kept interrupting his outright murder.

"Make room, dammit. How much am I payin' you to keep the fights out of my place? And that's not even mentionin' the free booze you swill." Chauncey's threat to cut off the marshal's largesse struck home.

"Don't worry your head none. I'll see that he sleeps it off. You need to get him to pay for any damage?"

"Taken care of, thanks for asking. He had a few nuggets in his pocket that ought to cover some of the cost," Chauncey said. The owner of the White Elephant Saloon growled like a wolf, kicked the fallen miner and then stormed out of the jail.

"In you go," Watkins said, opening the cell door and kicking the miner a few more times until he crawled inside. The cell door clanged shut. The marshal stared at his two prisoners for a few seconds, then muttered to himself and left.

Slocum figured the marshal wanted to find Latham or even Plummer and find out what to do now that there was a witness to any outright murder of Slocum.

"You get kicked around?" asked the miner. He had a breath strong enough to knock over a mule, but Slocum didn't shy away.

"Just had a shotgun aimed at my belly. Other than that, the marshal hasn't done much to me. Except letting his fleas gnaw on me." Slocum slapped at another of the jumping insects trying to escape retribution after biting him.

"Never seen a town where they'd toss a man in the clink for bein' drunk," the miner said. He scratched himself as fleas attacked his skin. From the look of the man, he might have brought some newcomers to the picnic.

"All I wanted was to ask a man about George Garson," Slocum said.

"Garson? That's not a name that sounds familiar," the miner said. "What's he look like? I make a point of buyin' every mother's son a drink when I get to town. Might be I've seen him."

Slocum related Jane's description the best he could, then perked up when he saw a flash of recognition cross the man's face.

"I seen him. Yeah, pretty sure I have. He's ridin' with a bunch of road agents. Least, I think that might be the gent from the way you described him. Real tough case, too. Dangerous."

"The gang that Luke Latham works for?" Slocum held back mentioning the marshal.

"Don't know Latham, but I saw this Garson fellow not a week back. I was workin' my claim and him and a dozen others came past. I noticed them 'cuz of the wagons they drove. Four heavily loaded wagons. Not something I see up in the hills."

"You ever hear of a town named Paradise?" asked Slocum.

"Nope, can't say that I have."

"Where's your claim? I don't mean to jump it, just want to find Garson." Slocum saw how reluctant the man was to give out such sensitive information. "I came across a huge gang a few miles from Quince's shebang," Slocum went on. He detailed its location.

"Might be Garson and the rest were headin' in that direction. It's not too far from where I've staked out my claim." The miner stared at Slocum, almost daring him to deny he had a proper claim. His bloodshot eyes blazed.

"Might be I can find out more about Garson by going back to the road agents' camp," Slocum said. He settled back, thinking fast. George Garson riding with the outlaws was both a benefit and a big inconvenience. Finding the gang would be easy enough, but cutting Garson out of the herd could be a real chore. Still, finding the man was what Slocum saw to be the hardest part of the search.

"You want to leave?" Slocum asked.

"Jail? The marshal's got no call holdin' me."

Slocum pulled his belt free from around his waist, looped it and went to the bars. A single cast roped the keys. He jerked fast and sent them sailing to land at his feet. Slocum took a few seconds to get his britches hitched up again, then picked up the keys and opened the door.

His cell mate rushed to the outer door while Slocum strapped on his gun belt and made sure the Colt Navy was loaded and ready. It didn't surprise him much that the chambers were all empty.

"Hold on," he called. "I need to reload." If he had escaped earlier and rushed outside with his six-shooter waving around, the marshal would have cut him down as easily as taking a potshot at a tin can sitting on a rail.

"Coast is clear," the miner said, peering through a crack in the door.

Slocum pushed past the man and saw only normal activity along Orofino's main street.

"Hope you find the mother lode," Slocum said, slapping the man on the shoulder. From the way the miner's eyes darted around, he was considering returning to a saloon for another drink rather than the hard work digging out the glittering metal from the ground.

"Thank you kindly, mister." The miner set off with an unsteady gait. Slocum didn't bother seeing what the man's choice was but it undoubtedly would be a saloon. Slocum went to the rear of the jail, found his horse, mounted and trotted from town, heading for Jane's shack.

To his surprise he found her there.

"How come you're not at work?" he asked.

Jane's eyes widened in pleased surprise seeing him. "Chauncey told me I could come in late today, if I'd work longer hours the rest of the week. Did Watkins let you go?"

Slocum laughed.

"I didn't think so. He wanted you dead, John. I could see it in his manner."

"He works for Plummer and his gang, but he's not got the stomach for murder. Watkins tried to make it look like I was escaping, but he didn't do it right. But that's not what I wanted to tell you." Slocum hurriedly told what the miner had related to him. He watched Jane's expression change until it carried such a mixture of emotions he couldn't keep them straight and doubted the woman could, either.

She was happy and sad, mad and fearful all at once.

"What are we going to do, John?"

"I'll ride out to the camp and do some spying. If I see your husband, you'll at least know he's alive. There might not be any good way of getting him to sign the divorce papers, though, if he's surrounded by a couple dozen of the road agents."

"If he's alive, it won't matter. I'll march right up and make him sign. I will, John, wait and see." Jane's determination sounded less like bravado than ignorance to Slocum.

"First, let me identify him. Then we'll figure out what to do." Slocum kissed her, the taste of her lips lingering on his as he turned to go.

He froze, hearing hooves outside the shack. Opening the door a crack sent a chill down his back. Marshal Watkins rode at the head of Latham and two others from Quince's shebang. It was a well-armed posse.

"You inside. Come on out or I'll open fire!" shouted Watkins, clumsily leveling a shotgun at the front door.

"John, what'll we do?"

Slocum didn't know, but they'd have to do it quick or Watkins and the others would fill the flimsy shack with lead.

10

"No!" Slocum cried, grabbing Jane by the arm and swinging her around. "They'll gun you down if you go out there."

"They've already seen your horse, John," she pointed out. "They know you're in here."

Slocum clamped his hand over the woman's mouth. Jane struggled, making it look more real. Slocum kicked open the door and thrust his gun out the door.

"I've got a hostage. Don't try to stop me!"

"Go on, cut 'em down," Luke Latham said, lifting his six-shooter, only to have it knocked aside by the marshal.

"Don't. You can't shoot a woman," Marshal Watkins said. Sweat beaded on his forehead and he looked as if he might lose his breakfast at any instant. Being a lawman wasn't the job he was best suited for.

"Why not? The bitch is in cahoots with him," snarled Latham. The other two outlaws started to take aim on Slocum but the marshal's warning had worried the rest of the men in the posse.

"That there's Miss Jane. She's not done nuthin' wrong. Don't hurt her, mister!" shouted the posse member.

"Everybody, down off those horses," Slocum ordered.

"Like hell!" Latham started to shoot but Watkins wrestled the man from the saddle to stop him. Slocum swung his Colt Navy around and fired at another of Quince's men, winging him. The man jerked back, dropped his six-gun and tumbled from the saddle. The other outlaw froze, his eyes burning on Slocum but aware how close he was to dying.

"Get down," Slocum repeated. The pressure of the townspeople forced the remaining outlaw to dismount.

"What now, John?" whispered Jane.

"Get on one of those horses. That one," Slocum said, pointing out the one Latham had vacated so abruptly. Watkins still stood over the man, keeping him from doing anything to harm Jane.

Slocum fetched his horse, mounted and joined Jane. He let out a loud cry, fired a couple times to get the horses galloping and left the posse on foot.

"Shoot him now!" growled Luke Latham. "He ain't got the damned bitch in his sights now!"

Slocum bent low as he put the spurs to his horse's flanks. The wind whipped past his face. From the corner of his eye he saw Jane using the reins to whip her mount along, too. After a mile, they slowed their breakneck pace and finally came to a brisk trot where they could talk.

"What now, John?"

"We need to get some help. Reckon Clint Bendix is healed enough to help us out?"

"Help us find my husband?" she said hopefully.

"Why not?" Slocum said. "Your husband might be riding with the outlaws who stole Bendix's cargo. Catch one, catch 'em all."

"I don't know if George could do something like that, but Latham was his friend and he's turned into such a low-down skunk! He called me a bitch! How dare he. I'll show him bitch!"

Slocum decided speed was their ally. It would take

Watkins and his posse a while to catch their horses. By then the marshal would have a dozen reasons not to pursue. If Latham and the other outlaws took it into their heads to follow, that reduced the number of men Slocum had to deal with. More likely, Latham would report to Quince and Plummer and ask what to do next. It wasn't absolutely certain but Slocum thought the danger was passed.

He still kept up a ground-devouring pace to cover the distance to Lewiston as quickly as possible.

But as he rode, he worried a bit about Latham's reaction. The man had to have recognized Jane if she was the wife of a good friend, a partner who had ridden with him all the way from Nebraska.

"Latham have something personal against you?" Slocum asked.

"What? No, not that I know. Now that you mention it, he was mighty vindictive, wasn't he? He wanted me dead. Or perhaps he only wanted me dead and you blamed for it."

"You'd still be dead. That doesn't set well with the idea of him and your husband being friendly."

"They might have had a falling out," Jane suggested.

That didn't feel right to Slocum either. If anything, Luke Latham would want to take up with the wife of an enemy to get even.

By the time they reached Lewiston, Slocum still hadn't figured it out.

"I'll bet Clint Bendix didn't stay in the hotel," Slocum said, eying the three-story structure. "Let's see what the livery stable has to offer."

They rode around the hotel and down a crossing street before they found the livery. Sure as rain, Bendix was sitting on a stool in the shade, arguing with the stableman.

"He won't give you a discount, no matter how long

you argue with him," Slocum said, leaning forward in the saddle.

"Discount? He's a thief! He's tryin' to charge me double for a new team of mules."

"I offered a durned good price. Take it or leave it," the stable owner said tartly.

"Let me talk to my, uh, banker," Bendix said. "In private." The stabler grumbled and went inside to tend to his chores. Bendix slowly got to his feet and walked over, favoring his right side. Other than stiffness, he looked to be in good condition.

"We need some help, Bendix," Slocum said.

"You need plenty more'n that," Bendix said. "Marshal Watkins sent a telegram to the sheriff sayin' you escaped his hoosegow. Don't know if Sheriff Allen put much store in it, but there's supposed to be a posse out huntin' you down." He looked over at Jane. "Might be after her, too."

"Could be," Slocum said, dismissing Bendix's report. He quickly explained how they sought Jane's husband and Bendix's stolen cargo.

"So your husband might be one of them varmints. Sorry to hear that, ma'am," Bendix said.

"Don't be sorry. All I want is for the snake to sign divorce papers, if he's still alive. Imagine him leaving me without so much as a fare-thee-well!"

"Imagine that," Bendix said, shaking his head in disbelief. He licked his lips, then turned to Slocum. "What do you want from me?"

"Supplies, ammo, maybe different horses. I want to start the search at the camp where you got shot. I'll need more than a six-shooter if I tangle with that many road agents again."

"Go on, change your horses. I got a few inside, ones that I wasn't cheated blind buyin'!" Bendix raised his voice enough for the liveryman to overhear. "Saddle me a horse, too. I'm goin' along."

"Are you up to riding, Mr. Bendix?" asked Jane.

"Ah, somebody who cares for my well-being. I jist wish I remembered your sweet ministrations when I was laid up. But yes, ma'am, I am fit as a fiddle if it means gettin' some justice."

"And your merchandise back," said Slocum.

"Them oysters are prob'ly dead by now. Hope them varmints pizzen themselves eatin' them. But the rest of my shipment won't spoil. And you're durned right that I want it all back."

Slocum was reluctant to let Bendix come along but saw no way around it. Unless Clint Bendix furnished the seed money and supplies, there was little chance of finding Jane's husband, dead or alive, or the outlaws responsible for the thefts of so much merchandise.

"Which horses can we use?" asked Slocum, giving in to Bendix.

"Who do you think them riders are, Slocum?" asked Bendix.

Slocum said nothing. Bendix and Jane both knew the answer as well as he did. He had been wrong about Marshal Watkins turning tail and hiding in his tiny jailhouse. The lawman had a full-blown posse out scouring the countryside for his escaped prisoner. That determination worried Slocum because it was more than likely fed by Luke Latham. Whether threats or outright bribery had been used didn't matter as much as a dozen men out hunting for him.

"We're close to the outlaws' camp," Slocum said. "Keep your eyes peeled for trouble."

"I was born ready for trouble," Bendix assured him.

Slocum wasn't so sure. The merchant had shown no sign of weakness as they rode, but now and then he turned and put his hand over his wound, signaling either stiffness or outright pain. A moment's hesitation in a gunfight meant somebody died.

Slocum hoped it wouldn't be any of them.

"Are you ready?" he asked Jane. Her lips thinned with determination, and when she pulled a heavy black-powder Remington six-shooter from her saddlebags, Slocum knew her resolve was set in stone.

"You know how to use that?" he asked.

"It was in the gear for this horse, but yes, John, I know. Want me to show you?" She hefted the three-pound gun and pointed it. Her aim didn't waver but he stopped her from firing.

"Be careful there," Bendix warned. "We don't want to alert them."

Slocum was more concerned about bringing the Orofino posse down on their necks than he was of spooking the road agents.

"Worst we can do is set the posse on the outlaws," said Bendix. "We'd be dealt out, no matter what happened."

"First, we're looking for Jane's husband."

"George Garson, I know, Slocum, I know. But don't let any of them destroy my wares. I need it or I'll go bankrupt. Bad 'nuff losin' the oysters."

"Maybe they kept them iced down," Slocum said, not believing that for an instant but saying it to forestall a long diatribe from Bendix. He studied the lay of the land and pointed. "Over there's where we found them before. In that grove of trees."

"I don't see any smoke from cookin' fires," said Bendix. "That's not a good sign."

"It's the middle of the afternoon. They wouldn't have begun preparing supper yet," said Jane. "How many would be in the camp, anyway?"

"No telling," said Slocum. He turned in a full circle, hunting for any trace of riders. The posse now made him as uneasy as tackling an entire camp of outlaws, because they were an unknown force. As many of them might be road agents as honest, decent men from town whom Slocum wouldn't want to shoot but might if they caught him in an ambush.

He'd willingly fill road agents with lead from sunrise to sunset, but men only doing what they thought was their civic duty presented a problem for him.

"Let's hurry," he said.

"Sooner's better," agreed Bendix, but for an entirely different reason. He was anxious to recover his loaded wagons.

They trotted into the grove of trees until Slocum silently motioned for them to halt. He listened hard but heard only the soft sigh of wind through the squat, leafy box elders.

"You want us to stay while you scout ahead?" asked Jane. Her nerves showed now. She held the heavy six-gun across her lap but looked less sure about using it.

"No need," Slocum said. He rode through the forest and came out into the clearing.

The deserted clearing.

"I'll be damned," groaned Clint Bendix. "They upped and left. Took all my merchandise with 'em, too."

Slocum rode slowly through the dusty area. The outlaws had camped here long enough for their horses to have cropped the grass short and then cut the sod with their hooves. A couple dozen men camped here would take the better part of a week to leave behind such a site. They had prepared their meals in four fire pits, and piles of garbage nearby showed their lack of camp sanitation and discipline. It was exactly what Slocum expected to find.

"Where'd they go?" asked Jane. "Can you track them?"

"The wagons left by that trail," he said, "but they rolled out at least a day ago. Might even have been right after Bendix got shot. That might have spooked them."

"Lollygaggin' ain't gonna find this little lady's hubby, and it surely ain't gonna find my wagons," Bendix said.

"Quiet!" Slocum cocked his head to one side.

"What is it, John?" asked Jane.

"Ride!" he cried. "Get out of here!" The command had barely left his lips when all hell broke loose and the air filled with flying bullets.

11

A bullet missed Slocum's ear by inches. He put his head down and galloped across the outlaws' campsite, looking left and right to see that Jane and Bendix flanked him. But by the time they got to the road taken by the outlaws driving off Bendix's wagons, Slocum saw he had only one companion.

"Where's Jane?" he called to Clint Bendix.

"Dunno," Bendix said, flailing about in the saddle like he was riding a bucking bronco. He almost tumbled from the saddle when another barrage sang past him, blowing splinters out of nearby tree limbs and sending a flurry of leaves into the air.

Slocum craned his neck as he tried to find the dark-haired woman. It proved impossible at such breakneck speed because the clearing quickly vanished behind a thin barrier of hackberry trees.

"I can't let the posse take her," he said, drawing rein. But the frightened horse, unused to having him in the saddle, refused to obey and veered off course rather than slowing. Slocum kept up the pressure on the bit until the frightened horse relented and slowed its gallop.

"Slocum, you cain't go back there. They'd cut you down and slice you up," Bendix said.

"What do you think they'll do to her?" demanded Slocum, but his first impulse was slowly overridden by good sense. Bendix was right. Riding back into the leveled guns of a posse led by Plummer's men was not going to help Jane. If they caught her, it would be a while before they figured out what they had and acted.

By then, Slocum could be in a position to stop them. If he didn't get himself caught or killed first.

"What're we gonna do now?" asked Bendix, finally regaining control of his horse.

"Keep riding," Slocum said. "There's a ravine a quarter mile from here that leads to a stream. We get there, follow it back and circle behind the posse. Then we can decide what has to be done."

"That's so," agreed Bendix. "Miss Jane might've got away, too."

Although Slocum knew that was possible, he didn't think it was likely. The posse had opened up on them from three sides, and he and Bendix had ridden away in the only direction possible to avoid being filled with holes.

Slocum led the way and thought he heard the posse thundering along the road, going away from them. He wondered if any of them could follow a trail. He hoped not, because this gave him and Bendix a few extra minutes' head start. When the posse reached a hill where they could look down over the countryside, they'd know their quarry had eluded them and would return at a gallop. By then Slocum wanted to be certain that Jane had not fallen into their hands.

"Slocum," said Bendix, "I saw somethin' up ahead. In the woods."

Blinking to get dust out of his eyes, Slocum pulled down the brim of his hat and scanned the line of trees.

"Ambush!" he called, jerking to one side. Rifles opened up on them. If Bendix hadn't spotted movement, they would have ridden smack into the trap.

Slocum and Bendix wound their way through the increasingly thick forest, then Slocum edged away from their general direction of travel to get to an area of the woods where speed might aid them again. He heard men crashing through the undergrowth behind them, cursing and carrying on.

"How'd the posse get all around us?" asked Bendix.

"There," Slocum said. "We can hide over there." He hit the ground, jerked out his rifle and led his horse into a small cleared space where someone had cut down a few trees for firewood. Bendix trailed more slowly, barely getting out of sight before their pursuers noisily appeared on their trail.

"I'll be goldanged," Bendix said, drawing his six-shooter. "Them's outlaws, not posse. I recognize that one from back at the shebang."

Slocum didn't bother reminding Bendix that the posse was probably being led by outlaws. But his friend was right about the men they spotted. Slocum didn't recognize all of them, but a few were from Quince's shebang. Then, when Quince himself rode out, he knew they had almost fallen into the road agents' ambush.

"Where'd they go?"

"Can't be far," answered one outlaw.

"You couldn't find your own ass using both hands," Quince snarled.

"You want to try to find it for me, Quince? Come on. Get down and let's have this out. I'm sick of your mouth."

Slocum lifted his rifle and had almost fired when Quince drew his six-shooter and gunned down the other outlaw, never giving his victim the chance to defend himself.

"If any of you galoots thinks to bad-mouth me, do it

now while I got my gun out. I don't want to waste time and energy drawin' a second time."

"He murdered him," whispered Bendix. "I figgered him for a back-shooter but . . ."

Slocum shushed Bendix and his outrage. He kept his rifle trained on Quince but hesitated to fire, although he had a good, clean shot. There were too many others with Quince to risk a shootout now. More than a dozen finally showed up and milled about, looking at their fallen companion but saying nothing directly to Quince about it.

A few made halfhearted attempts to find Slocum's and Bendix's trail and then gave up. Quince angrily ordered them back into the saddle and all rode off, continuing into the forsst. Slocum waited ten minutes before venturing out to examine the body of the outlaw they had left lying where it fell.

"Poor son of a bitch," muttered Bendix. "Should we bury him?"

"No," Slocum decided. "If Quince comes back, we don't want to give ourselves away." He dropped to one knee and rummaged through the man's pockets but found nothing to tell where the outlaws' new camp might be, or even who the man was. It was as if he had already been cleaned out.

"Then it'd make me mighty happy if we'd get to ridin', Slocum. There's nuthin' to be learned from a dead man."

"Reckon not," Slocum said. He mounted and they made their way back to the clearing where the road agents had their camp. The dust hanging in the air came from the posse galloping through and made it more difficult for Slocum to find the direction Jane had gone.

"This way," he said after almost twenty minutes of study.

Slocum looked up at Bendix. The man had turned as pale as bleached muslin and wobbled in the saddle.

"You shouldn't have come," Slocum said. "You're not healed yet."

"I had to."

"Get on back to Lewiston," Slocum said. "Find Sheriff Allen and tell him what's happened. I doubt he'll care much about the posse, but tell him the gents he had Marshal Watkins lock up for kidnapping are all loose and riding with the outlaws again. That'll light a fire under him."

"Allen don't strike me as the sort of gent to take kindly to anyone crossin' him," Bendix agreed. "The sheriff'll give me some satisfaction or I'll know the reason why." He clung fiercely to the saddle horn to keep from tottering.

"Go on, get out of here. You need to rest up before you can get back onto a horse."

"Always preferred to ride in a driver's box rather'n straddlin' one of these beasts," Bendix said, grinning sickly. "Thanks, Slocum. You find that li'l filly now, you hear?"

Slocum nodded, slapped Bendix's horse on the rump to get it moving and then turned to the trail he had found. With both the posse and the outlaws rampaging through the country, he wasn't sure Jane had a ghost of a chance of escaping capture or death. But as he rode across the broad valley and started into the higher country of the Bitterroots, his opinion changed. She had done a fair job of doubling back twice and had even tried to hide her trail by riding in a stream. He didn't find it unduly hard to track her, but the trailing skills shown by both miners from Orofino and the outlaws themselves was close to zero.

When the setting sun began casting long shadows in front of him, Slocum knew he would lose the trail in darkness. All afternoon he had followed her and hadn't caught

up. More important, he hadn't seen hide nor hair of the
outlaws or posse.

Taking a gamble, Slocum cupped his hands to his
mouth and shouted, "Jane!" The words echoed against the
rocky mountains and down a canyon until entirely swallowed by distance. He repeated his call, then listened in-
tently for a reply.

A gunshot brought him around, facing a butte. His eyes
worked up the sheer stone face until he got to the top.
Outlined in the sunset he saw a tiny figure waving frantically.

From this distance all he could tell was that it was a
woman. He began hunting for the winding rocky path that
led to the top. Finding and following it took the better
part of an hour. Slocum wished his horse had been a bit
more surefooted after the way it seemed to dislodge every
loose pebble along the trail, but he got to the top of the
butte in one piece.

"It took you long enough," Jane said, standing with her
hands on her hips. He couldn't see her face in the darkness
but knew she looked exasperated. The tone of her voice
told him that much.

"You hid your trail so good I had to backtrack a couple
times. That slowed me down."

"I shot it," she said unexpectedly. "I had to."

"What did you shoot?" he asked.

"My horse. I got up the back way. I didn't even know
there was a path on the front of the cliff, the way you
came. But the horse stepped between two large rocks.
John, the sound of its leg breaking was terrible. It . . . it
sounded like a dry twig snapping."

Slocum walked past her to a large, dark, still form. She
had expertly aimed the round behind the horse's ear to
put it out of its misery. He checked the horse's leg and
saw bright white bone sticking out of the flesh.

"You did what was necessary," he said. "If you hadn't

fired when you did, I wouldn't have found you. Did you hear me calling your name?"

Jane wiped her nose in a very unladylike way on her sleeve and shook her head. "I shot the horse."

"You had to do it," he repeated. "Have you ever killed anything before?"

"Not even a chicken. That sounds silly, I know, we're surrounded by things and people dying all the time, but I never had to, my family had lots of money, servants, oh, John, why's this happening?" She dropped the Remington and ran to him, burying her face in his shoulder. Racking sobs caused her entire body to quake, and he felt hot tears soaking into his shirt.

"You should have stayed in Lewiston," he said.

"No, I shouldn't," she said, shaking her head but keeping her cheek pressed to his chest. "I have to get free of George, and I have to do it myself. He treated me so terribly. He should never have done it. I should have listened to my pa when he said George was only after my money. But I didn't have any when we married because Pa cut me off. I was poor as a church mouse, but I thought I had a husband who'd support me."

Slocum held her tightly, understanding now why George Garson had upped and left. He had thought he was marrying not only a beautiful woman but a rich one. Jane's father had sense enough to take away the handle to the money pump. When Garson saw he hadn't tapped the mother lode the way he had envisioned, he abandoned her.

He was doubly a fool.

"I didn't find my husband," Jane said, sniffing loudly. She turned her face up to Slocum's. He kissed her, gently at first then with increasing passion. She held back but only for a moment.

Slocum felt her tongue force its way between his lips and surge into his mouth to tangle with his oral organ.

He sucked gently as her tongue remained, and then he pushed it out with the tip of his to enter her mouth. Back and forth they frolicked like frisky colts jumping from one pasture to another until both were panting with desire.

"Yes, John. It's right. Now, it's right."

Slocum could almost forget she was married. Her husband had done her wrong and was a fool to have wanted only money from a woman this lovely, this willing, this exciting.

They sank to their knees, kissing the whole way down. The grassy patch needed a blanket stretched over it but neither of them noticed. Their passions consumed them, and taking the time to get the blanket from the horse would have interrupted their exploration of one another's bodies.

Slocum was never quite sure how it happened but Jane got his shirt off and kissed and licked his chest, tangled the thick mat of hair there and then worked lower. As she moved down on him, he skinned her out of her blouse, leaving both of them naked to the waist.

"Such a lovely sight," he said, reaching down and cupping her breasts. He bounced them gently, as if he were taking the measure of a pair of melons. Then he caught the nipples and pinched down hard. This brought a moan of delight to the woman's lips.

"So nice," she said. "My whole body is on fire now."

He shut off her words by kissing her again as they both sank to the ground. A few more minutes of maneuvering got her skirt hiked and his jeans down so his manhood could spring out hard and free.

Slocum sucked in his breath when he felt Jane's fingers tighten around his turgid length. He ran his own hand between her legs, parted them and then worked up slowly, tantalizingly, until he found the dampness hidden away like a special treasure. His finger slipped easily into her and wiggled around until she squeezed down even tighter on his shaft.

"That's so good, John, but I want *this*." She tugged at his organ, pulling him toward the intimate recess they both wanted filled. "Hurry, hurry, you're driving me crazy!"

He wasn't about to rush. He licked and suckled at her tits and then kissed up to the woman's upturned chin. Her swanlike throat was exposed to his kisses, but Slocum didn't stop there. He worked to her earlobes and nibbled gently, kissed across her lips to her other ear and then— only then—did he swing his body around to position himself between her widespread legs.

"Yes!" she cried as he moved forward. Her hand guided him directly to the carnal bull's-eye. The tip of his fleshy column touched her nether lips, then surged fast and hard all the way into her.

Jane arched her back and cried out in joy as he buried himself fully inside her. Her rump lifted off the grass and her hips began grinding hard, driving her crotch into his. Slocum felt as if he was a spoon thrust into a mixing bowl. Hot, tight, moist, her female sheath surrounded him.

He grew to even greater proportions hidden away in her, then began pulling back. Jane reached up to claw at his arms, trying to hold him where he was. Slocum knew the momentary void would quickly be filled again. And it was. He raced back, this time grinding his hips into her. Then Jane lifted off the ground again and pressed firmly into him, their loins moving in opposite directions, striving for the ultimate in human pleasure.

They moved in this fashion for a delightful eternity, their emotions and sensations strung out to the breaking point. Slocum hung on only a few seconds longer than Jane. She screeched as her body trembled and shook in release. The pressures as her slick inner channel collapsed around him robbed Slocum of his control.

He felt as if he were a taut string that had been plucked. The tension deep within him built to the breaking point. He felt the hot rush and then a second tremor seize and hold the woman. Together they moved and thrilled to one another's body, and then it faded to a warm glow.

Slocum sank down on top of Jane, his face inches from hers. Her eyes fluttered open. Blue eyes stared at him as she whispered, "Wonderful, so wonderful, John."

"Want to bet?" he asked.

"Double or nothing?" Jane laughed in delight and then wrapped her arms around him as he kissed her and began working them both back to the lofty peak they had just visited. It took longer but neither objected.

12

"But we haven't found George," complained Jane Garson.
"I want to track him down."

"He's where we can't get to him, assuming that he's
still alive," Slocum said. "If he rides with the outlaws,
he's surrounded by a couple dozen nasty customers."

"It's all that Luke Latham's fault. He's the one who
led George astray," Jane said with conviction. She rested
her head on his back as they rode along. Slocum wished
they could make better time, but with both of them on his
horse, he didn't want to push the animal to the breaking
point unless—until—it was necessary. He had too many
people to flee without killing the horse before he ran afoul
of the outlaws or Marshal Watkins's posse.

"I've found that a man's not likely to do anything he
doesn't want to do," Slocum said slowly. "Your husband
could never have been talked into leaving you if that
hadn't been on his mind from the start."

"You're no comfort, John," the dark-haired woman
said. "At least you could lie to me. Tell me it's all Latham's fault and that George will rush back to me as soon
as his so-called friend is locked up." He felt her stiffen a

bit. "Or dead. I wouldn't mind seeing Luke Latham dead after what he said about me."

Slocum guided the horse through the clumps of trees, warily avoiding the road except for long stretches where he could be sure they weren't followed. The closer he got to Lewiston, the better he felt about Watkins's posse not finding them. But the road agents operated everywhere. It had taken iron will for him not to go to Quince's shebang and call out the men in it.

With Jane behind him, however, he had to play it safe. Even if Clint Bendix had ridden alongside, Slocum might have played it the same way. By himself, he'd take risks that the others might not tolerate, but that was the only way progress would be made against Quince and Plummer and their gang. Marshal Watkins was in their hip pocket and, as much as Slocum didn't want to believe it, there was a chance that Sheriff Allen was similarly bought and paid for.

"I've got to trust someone," he said more to himself than to Jane.

"You can trust me, John. I promise I'll never double-cross you," she said, snuggling closer. Her arms tightened around him, making him a trifle uneasy. He liked to have his arms free to move, to draw, to whip his horse into a gallop, should the need arise. Jane would only slow him down.

It took the better part of two days before they returned to Lewiston. Slocum rode into town from the west, having circled to throw off anyone tracking them. But he hadn't seen another living soul since he and Jane had spent the night on the butte in the Bitterroots.

"We ought to find Bendix," Slocum said, "but I'm more inclined to inquire after the sheriff. He should know what we found."

"You're going to tell him about George? Do you think he could help find that snake in the grass?"

"I doubt it, but there's chance he might have seen him in town, with Latham or some of the others in Plummer's gang. If so, that'll help Sheriff Allen identify the road agents."

Jane slipped her leg around, sat for a moment on the horse's rear quarters, then jumped lightly to the ground. Slocum was a bit stiff from riding, and it felt good to stretch his limbs once he had dismounted and tied the horse near the watering trough. He hitched up his gun belt, made sure the ebony-handled Colt was close at hand, then went to the sheriff's office.

Sheriff Allen looked up from his reading. He had a newspaper spread on the desk in front of him and a pencil in his hand.

"Wondered when you'd get back, Slocum," the sheriff said. "Your pal Bendix told me what you ran into out there."

"He tell you about Miss—Mrs.—Garson's husband?"

"He mentioned that in passing. His stolen goods occupied the bulk of what he had to say."

Slocum had to smile a little at this. That was Clint Bendix.

"Sheriff," Jane said, pushing past Slocum. "I want to find my husband and get him to sign some papers. Either that or I want to be certain he is dead."

"I might find a living body, but if your hubby's dead, proving it's him will be nigh on impossible." The sheriff cleared his throat and looked at Slocum, warning him not to go into more detail. A corpse left out in the open got eaten by a variety of varmints mighty fast, making it impossible to guess who it might have been.

"Go on," Slocum urged. "Describe your husband for the sheriff."

Allen listened politely as Jane detailed everything she could remember about her missing husband, but it wasn't until she mentioned Luke Latham that the sheriff perked up.

"Latham? This galoot?" Allen pawed through a stack of wanted posters and drew out a freshly printed one.

"Why yes, that's Luke Latham. See, John," she said, turning toward Slocum, "I knew Latham was a bad influence."

"What'd you say your husband's name was? George Garson?"

"Why, yes." Jane caught her breath. "You know something, don't you, Sheriff? And it's tied in with Latham."

"You recognize this one?" Sheriff Allen pulled out another wanted poster.

Slocum saw right away that Jane recognized the crudely drawn picture as one of her husband.

"I don't understand. This wanted poster isn't for George Garson."

"It's for George Plummer. Looks as if your hubby's taken a summer name."

Slocum was as surprised as Jane.

"Which is the false name?" Slocum asked. "Plummer or Garson?"

"I . . . I don't know," Jane said in a small voice. "Whatever it is, he lied to me. He's the leader of the gang stealing from all the wagon trains from here to Orofino? I never thought he had that kind of imagination or ambition."

"He's a dangerous one. Five-hundred-dollar reward," Sheriff Allen said.

Jane started to say something but no more words came out. She took a deep breath, turned and rushed from the sheriff's office. Slocum followed her into the street.

"What are you going to do?" he asked.

She turned to face him. Her azure eyes flashed hotly. "What I intended from the start. To get him to sign the divorce papers. Then I can turn the skunk in for the re-

ward!" With a swish of her skirts, Jane stormed off. Slocum wasn't sure where she was headed, but he knew she
had to be alone to work out this sudden turn of events.

He walked his horse back to the livery stable behind
the hotel and found Clint Bendix sprawled in a haystack
nearby sound asleep. Slocum didn't intend waking the
man, but Bendix's eyes flickered open and then he sat up.

"I was wonderin' when you and the purty filly'd get
back."

"You're not going to believe what's happened," Slocum said. "We found out that Jane's husband is still
alive."

"Do tell." Bendix looked closely at Slocum. "What
more ain't you sayin'?"

His reaction was about the same as Slocum's had been
when he found out.

"You want to ride along, Slocum?" asked Sheriff Allen.
"I've heard tell that a few of them outlaws are camped
alongside the road a couple miles outside town. Might be
that Plummer's with them."

"Are you sure of that, Sheriff?"

"Can't be sure of anything these days." Allen shook his
head, then spat a gob of tobacco. "A shame such a beautiful girl's tangled up with the like of George Plummer."

"Let's go," Slocum said. He had joined Bendix in the
haystack for a couple hours of sleep, but his friend still
slept the sleep of the righteous. Bendix looked stronger
than he had when he left Slocum and Jane out near the
old outlaw camp, but he still had a bit of mending to go.

"You want to let Mrs. Garson know where we're heading?" Allen asked. "Or should that be Mrs. Plummer?"

"Miss Jane's what they called her over at the Orofino
saloon," Slocum said. "That's as good as any other name
and better than most."

"I take it that means you're not going to bother her.

Smart. I've seen women happy and sad, but never in my born days have I ever seen one that angry. No telling what she'll do when she funnels that anger."

They rode at a canter from Lewiston, heading due east. The sheriff wasn't a talkative man, and this suited Slocum just fine. He had a powerful lot of thinking to do. If it came down to a shootout with Plummer, Slocum wasn't sure how Jane would react. Slocum didn't intend to be buried in any town's cemetery, not anytime soon. What would the woman think if he killed her husband? She said she wanted his scalp right now, but that was anger and hurt talking. Jane had some feelings for him once or she wouldn't have married him against her father's wishes.

Slocum decided he didn't want to stay around to find out what she'd say or do if it came down to a fight between him and Plummer, because the outlaw would be the loser.

"Up ahead's where the courier saw the men. He thought they looked suspicious, so I showed him a few posters. He identified two of them as being in Plummer's gang."

"What have you done to shut down the shebangs?" asked Slocum.

"Can't do anything without proof. If you hadn't lost those six wagons, that would have been hard evidence to use. We could have backtracked to Seattle and then investigated the supposed sellers in Coeur d'Alene. Somewhere along the trail Quince would have slipped up, and I'd have had him locked up."

"Like Jane's kidnappers over in Orofino," Slocum said.

"That's none of my concern. Marshal Watkins might be a crook but that's his town. I have to keep the county running. Just so happens Lewiston decided not to hire a town marshal, so I wear that badge, too."

"Didn't mean anything by it," Slocum said. He heard the right amount of outrage in the sheriff's tone to convince him Allen was a diligent, honest lawman. In Slocum's experience, those were rare traits for anyone wearing a badge.

"Smoke," Allen said, wrinkling his nose. He pulled back smartly on the reins, drew his six-gun and then looked to be sure Slocum was ready for a fight. "Suppose I ought to deputize you. So, consider yourself deputized, although I don't have a tin star for you to pin on your chest."

Slocum had no desire to be a deputy. Too often he was on the other side of the badge, but it felt good knowing he had some legal standing if they came on George Plummer in the camp.

As they rode closer, Slocum saw the men huddled around the fire. None of them was George Plummer. But Luke Latham went for his gun the instant he spotted Slocum.

Taking careful aim, Slocum squeezed off a shot that sent Latham's hat flying through the air. The nearness of the bullet rattled the gunman so much he got his six-shooter out but dropped it.

"I'll shoot you where you stand," Sheriff Allen shouted. "Hands in the air. All of you!"

The two men with Latham exchanged glances and Slocum knew they had a fight ahead of them. He winged one, hitting him in the upper leg as the man's six-shooter slid from its holster and the muzzle started upward to center on him.

"You shot me!" the man yelped. Slocum shot him again, this time in the arm so he would drop his gun.

Latham turned and ran, but the third man saw his partners out of action and two six-guns pointed in his direction.

"I give up. I was gulled by them, by Latham and Johnny there, the one with the bullets in him. I didn't want to rob them pilgrims on their way to Orofino."

"Shut up," grunted Johnny. "You don't need to spill your guts to them. They're the law. They'll hang us for highway robbery!"

"Not until you've had a fair trial," Allen said.

Seeing that the sheriff had the two covered, Slocum slid his Colt Navy back into his holster, unfastened the lariat bouncing on the side of his saddle and spun it into a loop. He had spent more years of his life roping strays than he cared to think about. Clutching down hard with his knees on the saddle to free his hands, Slocum started after Luke Latham.

Latham was on foot, and Slocum rode like the wind. He whipped the lasso over his head and then cast it expertly. It fell around Latham's shoulders as Slocum jerked back. His horse must have been used on a ranch for cutting because it dug in its hooves at the precise right instant.

Slocum might have seen a prettier sight than Luke Latham's feet flying up as the man suddenly became parallel to the ground but he couldn't think what it might have been. Latham crashed down so hard it knocked the wind out of his lungs.

Slocum wrapped the rope around the horn and dragged the outlaw back to where Sheriff Allen was putting the finishing touches on tying up the other two.

"Thank you kindly for bringing that one back."

"My pleasure, Sheriff," Slocum said. "What do we do now?"

"Got a complete confession out of this one," he said with pride. "These three yahoos are going to spend a bit of time behind bars for what they've done."

"Did he admit to anything more than robbing a few miners passing through?"

"That's crime enough for me," Allen said.

Slocum wasn't as pleased as the sheriff. Latham might

be convicted and sent to the territorial prison, but Quince and his boss, George Plummer, were both still on the loose. That was a condition Slocum couldn't allow to stand.

13

"They won't say a word about Plummer," Sheriff Allen said, dropping heavily into the chair at his desk. He hiked his feet onto the stained top and locked his fingers behind his head. "What are you going to do, Slocum?"

"Plummer's the leader of the gang. He's got a hefty reward on his head, so it looks as if I could kill three birds with one stone if I catch him and bring him in."

"Don't cotton much to bounty hunters," Allen said sternly. "But I'm not arguing with you about this. Those gents locked up in the back room are certainly close-mouthed about their boss. I don't for a second believe Latham is the one calling the shots. Too much robbing and outright swindling going on for a lamebrain like him to be responsible."

"Bendix's goods are long gone," Slocum said. "Have any of the stores here in Lewiston been offered champagne or other merchandise Bendix was shipping?"

"Can't say that they have. I'd check with Marshal Watkins, but you know what sort of answer I'd get from him. Everyone in Orofino could be robbed and he'd never notice."

"He ought to be sitting in the cell alongside Latham," Slocum said.

"Might be—one day."

"I'll scout around to find Plummer's new camp. There's no way I can tangle with that many road agents and ride away afterward without some serious injuries."

"When you find them, you hie on back, Slocum. I can round up enough decent citizens of Lewiston to deputize so we can take on a gang of twenty or thirty. Mostly, I've found that outlaws are a cowardly bunch. Seeing a posse equal to their number, they'll turn tail so fast they outrun even the jackrabbits."

Slocum left the county lockup and went straight to the livery stable to have a few words with Clint Bendix. Not seeing the merchant around, Slocum made certain his horse was well fed, then helped himself to the stack of provisions Bendix had put aside for their use in tracking down the outlaws. He considered leaving Bendix a note but saw no point in it. Either Bendix would figure out where he'd headed or he'd think Slocum had simply left for the coast, washing his hands of the whole affair.

Knowing Bendix the way he did, Slocum knew the mule skinner would never believe he had upped and left him in the lurch.

Slocum pictured the territory around Lewiston the best he could and decided Latham and the other two owlhoots had followed a stream down from higher in the Bitterroot Mountains. If they intended to rob a few miners on their way to the diggings and then retrace the path back so they wouldn't risk pursuit from anybody along the road, Slocum had a good idea where George Plummer might have moved his camp. It still surprised him the number of swindles and outright robberies George Plummer was involved in.

He spent a few minutes being sure he had several loaded cylinders for his Colt Navy stashed in his saddlebags. If he got into a gunfight, he would need all the firepower he could muster. Finally satisfied that he had all his ducks in a row, Slocum mounted and rode from Lewiston.

One day soon he had to spend enough time in the town to find out what it really had to offer. Then Slocum smiled. What did he need other than to spend some more time with Jane Garson? As this thought crossed his mind, he turned a bit dour. It wasn't right being with a married woman, even one intent on getting her husband to sign divorce papers, even one who had married an owlhoot like George Plummer.

Still, Slocum had done worse in his day. It might not have been right, but he had enjoyed himself and, from all he could tell, so had Jane.

"Penny for your thoughts."

Slocum jerked out of his reverie, hand darting for his six-shooter.

"You're jumpy, John." Jane stepped out from behind the thick trunk of a maple and stood, hands on her hips. She was dressed for the trail but there would never be any mistaking her for a man. Jane might have on a man's flannel shirt and jeans, but she filled them out in different, delightfully different, ways than a man would.

"That's a good way to get shot," he said. "What are you doing out here?"

"From the expression on your face, I wasn't who you expected to find. Or maybe that expression says I was. Were you thinking about me?" She was teasing but Slocum sat a little straighter in the saddle. Jane had hit close to home with that barb.

"I was thinking about your predicament," Slocum admitted, edging around what was actually running through his mind. Staring down at the woman brought back some of those thoughts. The top two buttons on her shirt were undone, revealing the white swell of her breasts just enough to distract him.

"Then we can ride along together and discuss it," Jane said.

"Wait," Slocum snapped. "You're better off going back to town."

"Of course I'm better off not being shot at or chased all over the territory," Jane said, "but sitting and staring out some window doesn't get things done. I want to find George and get him to sign the papers."

"There's more at stake than your divorce," Slocum said.

"I agree, but you have to start somewhere." To Jane this sounded reasonable. She got her horse and joined Slocum.

"How'd you know I was coming this way? I didn't know it myself until after the sheriff and I caught some of Plummer's men out on the road."

"News travels fast," Jane said. "One of Allen's deputies told me you had caught Luke Latham. The deputy was real nice and willing to pass along all manner of gossip. It didn't take long for me to decide you were going after the head of the gang, while the sheriff was content with snipping off a finger or two."

"A grisly way of looking at it," Slocum said.

"I have no problem with cutting the head off," Jane said, her voice grim now. "After I get his signature on the divorce decree, that is."

Slocum had to hand it to Jane and admired her single-mindedness. But she would also be in the way if he had to sneak into the outlaw camp.

"Ride along until I find them," Slocum said. "You can go back to town and fetch the sheriff and a posse."

"I—" Jane cut off her protest. "Very well, John. We'll proceed that way until the time comes."

He looked at her sharply, not sure what she was agreeing to. Jane rode with her bright blue eyes ahead and a tiny smile curling the corners of her mouth. Slocum wasn't her master and knew they could argue till hell froze over. It was simpler right now to let her come along.

"Latham isn't a good enough trailsman to do anything fancy. That's why I think his camp is somewhere along this stream. He followed it out of the hills to the Lewiston road, robbed a couple miners, and then intended to go back upstream."

"John," Jane said. "How many riders are ahead of us?"

Slocum turned and saw what she already had. He cursed under his breath for letting her distract him, but he hadn't thought he would find any outlaws for an hour or two. The look of the four men riding along the stream ahead of them almost screamed that they were on the run from the law. Slocum had seen the look before.

"They've spotted us," Slocum said. "Go on, hightail it. I'll delay them."

"There's someone behind us, too," Jane said, looking downstream.

Slocum saw they were sandwiched between two bands of hard cases. Running would bring both groups down on their necks, and shooting it out after being caught in the center was a sure way of becoming buzzard bait.

"We're going to have to bluff our way out," Slocum said. Jane nodded. She looked a trifle pale but otherwise didn't show her nerves.

Slocum slowed and let the two men behind them catch up. Dealing with a pair of outlaws would be easier than the four ahead, who kept riding. For a few seconds, Slocum thought they might be out of danger, then he saw that the men ahead of them had turned their horses and come back.

He faced six desperadoes.

"You headin' our way?" asked one of the men.

"Looks that way," Slocum said. He saw how both men eyed Jane. "How much farther is it?"

"Heaven's closer," grumbled the other man. "I got saddle sores from ridin' my ass off."

"You there. The four of you," called one of the riders who had been farther along the stream. "Where are you going?"

Slocum saw the other men hesitate. They weren't all in the same gang, in spite of them being on the run.

"Paradise," Slocum said, taking a shot in the dark. "We're going to Paradise."

"So're we. Let's go. We want to be there 'fore nightfall. Finding the way in is a bitch in the dark."

Slocum shot Jane a look to keep her quiet. They rode in silence, none of the men wanting to talk. That suited Slocum just fine. The less they said, the less likely they were to slip up and betray themselves.

At twilight, after a grueling climb into the Bitterroots, the gunman Slocum pegged as the leader held up his hand and signaled a halt.

"We're close to the cutoff," the outlaw said. "Remember, once we get in, there's no leavin' 'less we get permission. Everyone good with that?"

To leave now would attract unwanted attention. Slocum and Jane held their tongues. The two men who had been behind them argued briefly, then agreed. The leader wiped sweat from his forehead, settled his hat and then rode into what looked like a shadow. Only it swallowed him whole. The three hombres with him vanished, too.

"Let's go to Paradise," Slocum said to Jane. He urged his horse forward and quickly found himself in a rocky chute hardly large enough to accommodate his horse. Now and then he caught his shirt on the rocky walls. After almost twenty minutes of the closed-in riding he suddenly emerged into a broad valley. The darkness hid most of it, but nestled down below was a town blazing with streetlights.

"Paradise, yes, sir, a sight for sore eyes," said the out-

law who had led the way. "Everybody through? Let's go."
As he rode, he pulled out a bandanna from his saddlebags
and tied it around his left arm as a signal to some unseen
observer.

"Behind us," Slocum said, finally locating the guards.
"Two or three men with rifles on the mountainside."

"Your eyes are better than mine," Jane said. "I don't
see them."

Slocum wasn't sure he saw them as much as felt them.
If they had ridden through the narrow crevice and
emerged without giving the all-clear signal, they would
have been shot from the saddle. What had seemed bad
luck earlier now worked for their benefit. The man leading
the outlaws into Paradise had known the proper recognition sign.

"I never saw a town this prosperous in Idaho," Jane
said in wonder. "The streets are clear of garbage and look
at the lights! Gaslights as fine as any in St. Louis!"

Slocum had to admit he had been in meaner places.
Paradise had the look of a thriving town, but as they rode
down the main street he saw how different the citizens
appeared than in most towns. Orofino looked like a boomtown with rough-hewn characters. Here everyone either
wore a six-shooter strapped to his hip—or shackles.

"They don't kill intruders, they make them slaves," Slocum said. "No wonder the garbage is gone and the floors
are swept."

"How awful!" exclaimed Jane.

"Quiet," he warned. "We want to blend in. If anyone
asks, we're on the run from the law."

The small group stopped in front of what looked like
a jailhouse. Looking inside, Slocum saw that the cell
doors were all removed, making the hoosegow a parody
of a real one.

Like flies to shit, men poured from the buildings to look
over the newcomers.

A giant of a man waddled forward, chest thrust out and looking tough enough to wrestle a grizzly—and win.

"Who are ya and why're ya in Paradise?" he called.

"Me and my boys are dodgin' the Army," answered the man who had led them to this outlaw town. "We robbed a payroll over at Fort Lapwai, killed an officer and got the cavalry all riled at us."

"Heard tell 'bout that," the huge man said. "You and yer gang're welcome in Paradise."

Slocum and Jane remained in the saddle as the first four robbers dismounted. Slocum saw how the town population went for their six-guns when the two others also tried to dismount.

"Not you, not yet. What'd you do?" demanded the giant.

"I, uh, we're on our way to Canada. Just passin' through," said the man who had first spoken to Slocum back at the stream.

"What kinda law's huntin' for you?"

"None, not really, we—"

The crowd rushed forward and dragged the men from their saddles.

"Put 'em in chains and work 'em till they drop. Then we might see 'bout havin' some fun with 'em."

Jane made a small choking sound when she saw the two who had been with them knocked to the ground and put into shackles.

"What 'bout you?" the man asked belligerently. He glared at Slocum, who returned his gaze coldly.

"What about you?" Slocum countered. "Who are you to ask me anything?"

A buzz went through the crowd. They had heard bravado before and appreciated the show that had to follow. Slocum knew he had to do more than put up a bluff.

"The man who'll tell his friends to chain ya up." The giant looked over Jane. "Mighty fine travelin' companion you have. Be right pleased to chain her up, too."

"I killed a judge and his bailiff," Slocum said. "But it was a fair fight. I let them go for their guns before I shot them."

This took the giant by surprise. Then he let out a deep belly laugh.

"You got sand, I'll give you that. But who cares if you kilt a dozen judges?"

Slocum jumped to the ground and walked up to the man. The giant was a good four inches taller than his six feet and had a hundred pounds on him. None of it was fat.

"Are you calling me a liar?"

Silence fell.

"You got a death wish, don't ya?"

Slocum knew his death warrant would have been signed if he hadn't stood up to the man.

"You talk big, as big as that gut of yours, but that's about all that's big," Slocum said.

The giant roared in anger and swung a fist the size of a quart jar. If the blow had landed, it would have broken Slocum's neck. But Slocum expected the attack and ducked. He felt the wind from the fist against his cheek.

He set his feet, then landed four hard, fast punches to the man's belly. It felt as if he punched an oak tree.

"You'll have to do better'n that if ya want to do more'n annoy me."

Slocum was backpedaling when the man punched again. Slocum robbed most of the force by his movement but still felt as if he had been slammed in the chest by a sledgehammer. He got his balance back and knew a bare-knuckle fight could go on for hours, if the rules called for a new round to start after every knockdown. But this fight would end the first time his opponent landed one of his haymakers.

Slocum blocked a jab with his arm, staggered a little,

then waded in, whaling away at the giant's midriff again. He knew better than to land a blow on the man's jaw. That only broke knuckles. This time Slocum felt the abdominal muscles weaken just a little.

Not enough.

He dodged two more punches and saw his chance when the man was off balance. Slocum hammered away with a flurry of blows directly over the man's heart. A strange gurgling sounded, and it was the massive man's turn to stagger. Slocum never let up. He punched until his arms felt as if they would fall off, then he kept going until a final blow buried his fist wrist-deep in the man's belly.

With a whoosh, the air blasted from the man's lungs. He doubled over, giving Slocum his chance. He lifted his knee as hard as he could into the man's chin and snapped the shaggy head back. The giant fell to the street, out cold.

Panting, hands on his knees as he tried to get his breath back, Slocum looked up and saw the outlaws drawing their six-shooters and aiming them at him.

He had won the fight and lost the war.

14

Slocum sucked in his breath and tried to quiet his racing heart. He looked down the barrel of a six-gun no matter what direction he turned. Even if he could draw fast enough, he'd never bring down more than one or two.

"Who's next?" he asked. For a moment the world turned graveyard silent. Then excited chatter broke out all around him and the outlaws began putting away their guns.

"Never seen a gent who could deck Indian Burt like that," said one rat-faced outlaw, coming to slap Slocum on the shoulder before moving on. The rest of the crowd shared this opinion.

Slocum jerked when he felt someone moving close behind, but it was only Jane.

"Shouldn't you help him up?" she asked, staring at the fallen giant in the dust. Blood trickled from the corner of the man's mouth and turned to mud.

"Why?" Slocum grated. "If I did, they'd brand me a coward." He rubbed his knuckles and knew he had gotten lucky by finding the massive outlaw's soft spot. If he hadn't gotten a decent punch in over the man's heart,

115

Slocum would be the one lying in the dirt. Or worse. He might be six feet under by now.

"I need a drink," Jane said in a small voice.

As they went to the nearest saloon, everyone greeted them like long lost relatives.

"Come right on in and have a bottle of champagne," the barkeep called. "Just bought a few cases of it." He pulled out a bottle and set it on the bar in front of Slocum, who eyed the label.

"Good booze," he said. "I recognize it."

"You mean it's . . . ," Jane began before catching herself. Slocum nodded. It was Clint Bendix's champagne. George Plummer had brought it to Paradise after he had stolen it at Quince's shebang.

Slocum dropped a twenty-dollar gold piece on the counter, not expecting any change and not getting any. He popped the cork and took a drink, then passed it to Jane. Then groping hands took the bottle from her and the champagne was passed around the saloon.

"Good," Slocum said. "That's mighty fine bubbly wine."

The barkeep beamed in pleasure, then used Slocum's endorsement to sell the rest of the case to the outlaws. The noise rose until the swinging doors were pushed open. Filling the door frame, Indian Burt supported himself against the sides.

"Who was the judge?" he asked, his jaw waggling from side to side.

"Somebody who needed it," Slocum said. This brought a new round of laughter, and merriment spread through the room. Slocum watched closely as Indian Burt lurched to the bar and leaned heavily on it.

"Never been hit like that before, not even when a mule kicked me in the head," Indian Burt said.

"He's one tough hombre," Jane piped up, then regretted it because it drew Indian Burt's attention to her.

"And yer mighty purty. Anybody put a brand on you?"

Slocum started to slip between the woman and Indian Burt, but she spoke before he could.

"George Plummer's my man," she said.

"Plummer? Do tell," Indian Burt said, new admiration in his piglike eyes.

"Where is he? He's supposed to be around Paradise, isn't he?" she asked.

"He's out right now, pickin' up some more supplies. Ought to be back in town in a day or two."

"Good," she said with feeling, but Slocum hardly shared her pleasure.

"Yep, I run the town for him when he's out. I'll take real good care of you," promised the giant.

"There's no need," Slocum said. "I can do that."

"You a friend of Plummer's, too?"

"We've done business," Slocum said.

"Shoulda tole me straight out. Any friend of Plummer's is always welcome here. He don't own the place, but he might as well. He brings us supplies and keeps the law at bay. We're snug as bugs in a rug here cuz of him."

"How many citizens in Paradise?" asked Jane.

"We got damn near three hundred," Indian Burt said. "No law's ever found this valley, not what lived to act on the discovery. Every man here's wanted for some crime, 'cept the ones like those fools who came in with you."

"The ones you chained up?" asked Slocum.

"We don't want to do any of the work around here. It's too much fun drinkin' champagne, gamblin' and whorin'. Now and again a miner or sodbuster blunders into our valley. We work 'em till they die, then get some more to replace 'em. Plummer's promised a wagonload of mule skinners one of these days. Tough bastards, they are. Be fun seein' how much they can take 'fore they give up the ghost."

Indian Burt drifted off to drink with friends at a poker

table, letting Slocum and Jane talk in private.

"Sheriff Allen'll need a couple companies of cavalry to clean out this den of thieves," Slocum said. "I need to do some mapping so they can plug the exits."

"Exits? You think there's more than one way into town, John?" asked the dark-haired woman.

"Plummer is too sharp to let himself be bottled up. There're probably a dozen ways in and out. If Allen is going to catch a fraction of the road agents hiding out in Paradise, he needs to know where those passages are."

They went to the door and into the main street. Gas-lights hissed and popped the length of it. The buildings showed a level of prosperity not found in any other Idaho town Slocum had seen. Crime paid. Well.

"Where do you start?" she asked.

"It's dangerous for you, but I can work faster if I leave you here. You might find a hidey-hole and not come out until I get back."

"They're not any different from the miners who come into the White Elephant Saloon," Jane said, looking back into the gin mill.

"Most miners don't wear six-guns—and most won't kill you if you say anything the least bit suspect. They're a suspicious, high-strung lot inside."

"You're right, John. I'd feel safer if I came with you."

He chewed on this a moment, then said, "If we both record what we can, we can be out of here twice as fast. You sketch out the buildings in the town and try to find where Plummer stays, where his arsenal is, where he might keep his loot." Slocum doubted the wily outlaw left anything of value behind in a criminal haven like Paradise, but he wanted to keep Jane busy.

"All right, John, but you be careful." She hastily kissed him, then picked up a discarded newspaper and ripped it in two, giving him half and taking the other. Slocum didn't know what he would use to draw with but he'd find something.

He hurried across the street and ducked behind the buildings, checking alleys and noting several fortified two-story towers where a rifleman might hold off a small army. Slocum circled the town and found several of the secure structures, then backtracked from them to where ammo and rifles were cached.

He rubbed his forefinger across the newsprint and got enough ink on it to make smudges showing the location of the strongholds. As he walked around, the notion hit him that the way out of Paradise was likely underground.

The only building that looked as if it had been built on solid rock was the bank. Considering the distances and probable work needed to dig tunnels, Slocum began drawing what he thought would be the underground escape route from the bank.

A heavy hand spun him around and another grabbed at the paper.

"He's drawin' pitchers of the bank!" cried an outlaw.

The two owlhoots with him peered over the man's shoulder and immediately recognized how Slocum had mapped out the reinforced positions around Paradise.

"Yer a spy!" cried one.

"But he knocked out Indian Burt. And he kilt a judge!"

"He only said he killed a judge," said the third. "And we all knew Indian Burt'd find his match someday. It just happened to be a low-down snoop for the law!"

Slocum never moved a muscle, because the three hadn't come alone. Four others, all with their guns trained on him, made sure of that.

He couldn't help marveling at the irony of Marshal Watkins's posse after him for jailbreak and now he was caught by outlaws.

"Plug 'im. Shoot 'im where he stands."

"That's too good for a spy," argued another. The outlaws put their heads together and spoke in heated tones for almost a minute before coming to a conclusion. Slocum knew by the smirks on the men's faces that he wasn't going to like what they had decided.

"That way, mister. We're gonna have some fun 'fore you die."

Slocum let them take his six-shooter and shove him along to the outskirts of town. He tried not to be obvious as he looked around for Jane. She was nowhere to be seen. He hoped she had grabbed her horse and got out of Paradise as fast as she could ride. She might not make it past the sentries, but a rifle bullet was a cleaner death than anything else she was likely to get in this outlaw haven.

"Here, stop here," ordered one of the men, with his six-shooter aimed at Slocum's spine.

"What now?" Slocum asked. The man stepped up and shoved him a step back. "That's the best you can do? I'll fight you like I did Indian Burt."

"Yeah, sure," the outlaw said, shoving Slocum again. This time as Slocum stepped back, his foot found no support. He teetered on the edge of the pit, then tumbled down, arms flailing. He landed hard in a ten-foot-deep hole.

Shaking himself, he pushed to hands and knees and then dusted himself off as he stood. The men ringed the pit, their faces hidden in shadow. Slocum threw up his hand to shield his eyes when a sudden flare from a torch blinded him. The men brought up a half dozen torches and shoved them into the ground around the pit so it was as bright as day where he stood at the bottom.

As his eyes adjusted to the brightness, he picked out individuals now. They looked even more excited than they had before, making Slocum turn cold in the gut. They knew something he didn't.

"No!" he shouted. "Don't!" The crowd roared at his

apparent cowardice, but Slocum had seen Jane's face poking over the edge of the pit. She wanted to do or say something to save him. He couldn't let her. Whatever the fate the road agents had thought up for him must not be shared with the woman.

"You got old Tick?" asked one man.

"Right here, got the rabid son of a bitch right here."

Slocum was ready for anything but what happened. One instant the faces peered down. Then a hole appeared in the ring, suddenly filled with a snapping, growling bulldog. The men tossed the dog into the pit with him—and the dog was pissed.

Slocum reached behind and found the knife he carried sheathed there. He wished he still had his six-shooter, but even a few hunks of lead wouldn't have stopped the mad rush as the dog launched itself for his throat.

Sidestepping, Slocum let the dog bound past. But the animal hit on its stubby legs, spun like a top and attacked again in jig time, this time snapping for his legs. Slocum slashed downward with his knife, trying to sever the dog's spine. All he did was open a gash on the muscular flank. The bulldog hardly noticed.

The pain that shot through Slocum's leg as the dog clamped its powerful jaws on it was felt, though. For an instant, Slocum's world went red with the pain, then he stabbed downward again. The tip of the knife raked the dog's other side. Then Slocum lost his only advantage. The dog switched from his leg to his arm. Slocum felt the strength fade in his grip as he lost the knife.

He tried to get under the dog's throat to choke it. Heavy slabs of muscle protected it. With the dog hanging on, Slocum began battering it from side to side, smashing it into the dirt walls of the pit. The pressure on his arm never slackened.

From above came cheers and guffaws. Slocum knew they had been betting against him—no one thought he would win. The bets were on how long he stayed alive.

"John, John, here!"

Slocum looked up to see Jane's fear-racked face again. She tossed something into the pit. Using all the power in his shoulders, Slocum slung the dog around, then fell heavily to the floor. Inches away was his Colt Navy. He fought to move closer, but the dog continued to tighten its jaws on his arm.

The pain that had once surged now faded into dullness. Slocum knew shock was setting in. His left hand found the gun. Somehow he cocked the six-shooter and pointed it between the dog's eyes. The report was deafening but the dog didn't loosen its death grip. Slocum fired again and again before realizing the bulldog was dead.

Still it clung to him.

The men above began jeering and accusing one another of cheating. Slocum shoved the six-shooter into its holster and picked up his knife. It took several desperate slashes before he could cut the powerful tendons holding the dog's jaw enough to get it to release.

Cessation of pressure brought a new torrent of pain. Slocum swallowed hard and tried to ignore it. He could barely flex the fingers on his right hand, but they still moved. A little. The dog had left bloody bite marks but hadn't done any permanent damage.

Slocum felt weak in the knees and sat heavily, looking up. He expected to see the men lining up to take turns shooting him but the torches showed nothing. The outlaws had left.

It took him another minute for the sorry truth to settle in. Jane was gone, too.

15

Slocum did the best he could to bind the bite on his arm. His leg was stiffening but not too badly because his boot had taken the brunt of the bulldog's powerful jaws. After he patched himself up, he stepped to the center of the pit and looked for any way out. The brightly burning torches made him squint, but he didn't see anyone at the edge of the hole who might help.

He was as alone as if he had been dropped into the middle of the Mojave Desert. And he knew why.

Feeling the urgency of the situation, he went to the side of the pit and used the knife to dig a hole large enough for him to step into. He scraped out three more and then got halfway up and out of the pit before finding that he couldn't balance well enough to dig the needed holes for the last few feet to freedom.

Slocum fumed as he heard distant laughter and jeers. This spurred him to climb up the footholds again. This time he took the knife in his right hand and reached as far above him as he could, driving the knife into the side of the pit. He jumped, feeling the strain in his weakened arm. He pulled with all his strength, flopped around, scrambled as furiously as possible and lunged. His left

123

hand slipped over the lip of the hole. Flailing around, he caught one of the torch handles and grabbed tight.

Wiggling, struggling, almost falling, he pulled himself up and over the edge of the pit. He lay facedown on the ground, panting harshly. Being high up in the Bitterroot Mountains didn't help air reach his straining lungs, but he had exerted himself to the breaking point—and beyond. All he wanted to do was lie there on the cool earth and recuperate.

What he had to do was save Jane Garson.

Slocum got to his feet, worked clumsily to reload his Colt Navy so it carried six full chambers and then headed for the middle of town, from where the tumult echoed away to him.

No one noticed as he peered in the saloon window. If the three hundred outlaws in Paradise had crowded inside, it wouldn't have surprised Slocum. A couple sticks of dynamite would have saved many an executioner's fee. They would also have blown up Jane.

The men had lifted her onto the bar and were tearing bits from her blouse. No matter how she turned and twisted, an outlaw was there to steal a few more threads. She was almost bare to the waist, to the crowd's immense entertainment. She covered her breasts, but this prevented her from keeping the men from slowly cutting away at her jeans. Before long she would be buck naked.

Then the men's real fun would begin.

"I know George Plummer," she cried, trying to stop the torment. "I'm his wife!"

This produced a round of laughter that rattled the beams in the saloon ceiling.

"Sure you are," shouted an outlaw. "And I'm his mistress!"

"George wouldn't bed anyone as ugly as you. He's got better taste than that," Jane shouted, still trying to divert the men. She didn't succeed.

Slocum knew he had to do something quick. But what?

He turned to find where Paradise penned up its slaves. He might free enough of the men to provoke an attack. Slocum knew he could never whip the men who had been so badly abused into a fighting frenzy—he wanted to use them as a diversion. That was cruel to use them as cannon fodder, but all he could think of was saving Jane.

Before he had gone a dozen yards, five men rode down the middle of the main street. Slocum saw their faces clearly in the flickering gaslight.

"Plummer!" he called, but the outlaw didn't hear him. He was too intent on the crowd in the saloon. Slocum started after him, then slowed and finally went back to his spot at the saloon window.

He might not save Jane, but Plummer would when he saw who the citizens of Paradise were harassing.

"What's going on in here?" barked George Plummer.

The sudden silence was not as amazing as the way the crowd parted all the way to the bar where Jane stood, still trying vainly to hide her nakedness.

"Hello, George," she said. "Your friends were showing me a real good time."

"You!" Plummer bulled his way forward, reached up and grabbed her by the arm. He dragged her to the floor and shook her like a terrier shaking a rat. "What are you doing here?"

"Trying to find you, you low-down, no-account skunk!" Jane shouted back.

"You two fight," shouted someone at the back of the saloon. The call was taken up by others until George Plummer swung on them, drew his six-shooter in a lightning-quick move and fired into the ceiling.

"Shut your yaps," he said in a deadly voice.

"Is she really your wife?" asked the barkeep, bolder than most.

"I am!" cried Jane.

"None of your concern," snarled Plummer. He grabbed her by the arm and yanked her toward the back of the saloon. Slocum's view was blocked by dozens of men crowding around to get a better look. Any diversion in the town was something worthwhile to them.

Slocum backed off and looked around the side of the saloon, wondering if he could catch up with them. It wouldn't be long before the men remembered their prisoner in the pit and went back to torment him some more. They wouldn't take kindly to finding the pit empty, save for their dead fighting dog.

"You . . . you . . . you!" raged Jane. Slocum peered around the edge of the saloon into the back alley in time to see her standing, naked to the waist, sputtering at something Plummer had said. Before Slocum could make his presence known, Jane leaped at her husband, clawing for his eyes.

Plummer batted her aside, knocking her to the ground.

"I should have killed you rather than just leaving you."

"I loved you!" wailed Jane. "How could you ride out like that?"

"You were broke. I thought I'd steal a pile of money from your pa, but you were too dumb and did something to make him cut off your money."

"I *was* stupid," Jane sobbed. "I married you! That's why he wouldn't give me one red cent. He hated you. I should have listened to him rather than to my heart. I loved you, George, I loved you and—" Jane's words ended in another meaty thud as Plummer hit her.

Slocum swung around the corner, but found his way blocked by the four men who had come to town with him. He wasn't going to be deterred when the woman was being abused. Slocum slipped his pistol from its holster and buffaloed one outlaw. The man sank to the ground without making a sound. But the other three were alerted and spun on Slocum.

He had started to shoot the closest one when the outlaw to his left hit him hard. Slocum staggered, dazed. The road agent hit him again, harder this time. The world turned black as Slocum fell facedown into the dirt.

Tiny shards of sound scrapped at Slocum's brain. As if a thousand miles away he heard, "Just some drunk. Leave him. I got to build up the gang. Take her off my hands, will you?"

A roaring sound in Slocum's ears prevented him from hearing where Plummer had ordered his henchman to take Jane. Then soft, warm night crept up and enveloped Slocum.

Slocum awoke to pain. At first he lay on the ground confused and hurting. Then anger burned through his misery and he struggled to stand. Legs shaky, he propped himself against the saloon wall and looked around the alley. He was alone, but inside the saloon he heard boisterous laughter and the tinkling sound of a poorly played piano.

He should have taken out all four of Plummer's men and then stopped the gang leader from harming Jane. He should have, but his arm hung weak and limp at his side and his head felt three sizes too big. Slocum took a few more minutes to regain his strength, then went into the saloon to see if he could find Jane.

Nobody paid him any attention. They gathered around the piano, singing bawdy songs off-key and swilling a never-ending river of whiskey. As quickly as one bottle vanished down a thirsty gullet, another was passed from behind the bar.

George Plummer sat in a chair and presided over the festivities, controlling them like a conductor directs an orchestra. Slocum considered his chances of getting to the outlaw leader and forcing him to tell what had happened to Jane. He quickly discarded this as fuzzy thinking caused by getting hit on the head. A henchman sat to either side of the boss, and two positioned themselves behind to prevent Plummer from getting shot in the back. Slocum would be dead a dozen times over before he could reach Plummer.

Men went to Plummer, and were either turned away by his bodyguards or permitted to sit at the table for a few minutes. Whatever went on, the newcomer talked rapidly and Plummer listened. Some men left with smiles; others left looking as if they had found out they were being hanged at dawn.

"What's going on?" Slocum asked a jovial drunk who staggered by.

"T-thass recruitin' t-time," the drunk slurred. "Sure do wish I could sign on. Plummer pays t-top d-dollar." With that he bounced off another outlaw, received a punch to the jaw for his clumsiness and fell to the floor, his glassy eyes staring up at the ceiling.

Slocum found a chair and sat in it, drew his Colt and kept it pointed in Plummer's direction under the table in front of him. He wasn't sure what he could do about a room full of drunken thieves and killers, much less with four clear-eyed guards on all sides of the man he wanted to shoot.

After ten minutes, Plummer had cherry-picked the best—the worst—of the outlaws in Paradise. He had given the chosen ones a hefty bonus to keep them in his camp, undoubtedly promising them even more when they actually got out on the road to rob miners and to run the shebangs.

A fight broke out near the piano. Slocum turned slightly to make certain it wouldn't spill over into the corner of the saloon where he watched and waited. Two men went at it, bareknuckle style. They were both drunker than lords and spent more time falling down than they did hitting their opponent. The betting was fierce for the short time the fight lasted.

The two men collapsed into each other's arms, one supporting the other. They gave up when a new bottle of champagne from Clint Bendix's stores was passed around.

Slocum turned his attention back to George Plummer. His heart skipped a beat when he saw that the outlaw leader had left during the brief fistfight. Standing, Slocum held his six-shooter down at his side as he made his way out of the saloon and into the brightly lit street.

Plummer had vanished like a ghost.

Slocum took a deep breath, then stalked down the street, eyes scanning left and right for any trace of Plummer or his bodyguards. Where he found one, he would find the other. Plummer had a healthy dread of what the men hiding out in this town could do.

He came to a halt when he saw two of Plummer's men sitting with their backs to a wall and passing a bottle between them. Cautiously approaching, Slocum eavesdropped enough to know that they were waiting for Plummer and the other two bodyguards. As careful as he had been, the men looked up. One lifted his six-shooter and pointed it in Slocum's general direction.

"What do you want?"

"Some of that whiskey," Slocum said, pointing with his left hand while putting his right thumb on the trigger of the gun still hidden beside him.

"Get your own," snarled the outlaw.

"I've got a message for Plummer. Where'd he get off to? I saw him in the saloon but he lit out so fast, I didn't have a chance to deliver it."

"I'll give it to him," said the outlaw holding the bottle.

"Only to him. It's from Luke Latham," Slocum said.

"That stupid son of a bitch is in the hoosegow over in Lewiston," said the other, the one holding the six-shooter. He was suspicious but glanced to his partner. This brief inattention cost him his life.

Slocum lifted his pistol and fired into the man's head.

He died before he knew there was trouble. The other road agent dropped his bottle and fumbled for his six-gun.

"You'll join him if you try," Slocum said.

"You murdered him."

"He was going to kill me, wasn't he? Weren't you?" By including the second outlaw, Slocum had made it clear how easy it would be to fire another round.

"No, no, he wasn't going to do any such thing. I wasn't, either. I just wanted to get a snort or two of whiskey."

"Where's Plummer?"

"He . . . he's at his place. Second floor of the hotel. That's it down the street."

Slocum knew what the man was trying to do and played along by feinting. The instant it appeared that he was going to look in the direction the man pointed, the outlaw went for his gun. Slocum shot him, too.

No one could have heard the two gunshots over the uproar in the saloon. Slocum kept walking, this time with his destination in plain sight. He doubted the outlaw was clever enough to lie about Plummer's location, especially since he was thinking so hard on back-shooting Slocum.

The hotel didn't look any different from a hundred others Slocum had seen, but this one had Plummer's two bodyguards sitting in the lobby, swapping lies. A clerk behind the counter looked like a real hard case and had a sawed-off scattergun close at hand.

Slocum went around to the rear and saw a back stairway leading up. He took the steps two at a time, tested the door and found it locked. A quick kick opened it. Slocum drew his six-shooter and pointed it down the hall, waiting to see if Plummer's guards came rushing up from the lobby.

The sounds from other rooms made Slocum think this was more of a whorehouse than a hotel. He took a deep breath when he realized that was probably why Plummer had brought Jane here.

He walked the length of the corridor examining each door. The one at the end of the hall was made from polished maple and looked to be the presidential suite. If Plummer was anywhere, it would be there.

Slocum gingerly tested the doorknob and was surprised to find that the door wasn't locked. He twisted quickly and surged into the room. His gun swept from one side to the other and back.

Empty.

But the bedclothes were in disarray, telling Slocum what had gone on.

"Hey, Boss, you back so soon?"

Slocum pressed flat against the inside wall and waited. The clerk stuck his head in and Slocum swung his Colt Navy, catching the man just above the ear. He fell heavily to the floor, stunned and flopping about spastically.

"Where'd Plummer go? Where's Jane?"

"Mountains. Went into the mountains with her."

"Which direction?"

"Dunno."

Slocum believed him. He swung his six-shooter again and knocked out the clerk. Stepping over him, Slocum left the room and the hotel. He had a real chore ahead of him, trying to track a slippery outlaw and rescue Jane.

16

Slocum found his horse and gear at the outskirts of town in a community corral. He eyed the other horses and considered letting them all out, then decided against it. While it would afford some measure of revenge on the outlaws who had tortured him by throwing him into the pit with the bulldog, it would also alert them that something was amiss. He wanted to get on Plummer's trail as quickly as possible and not have to watch his back. Nobody tolerated a horse thief, not even other horse thieves.

Letting the horses loose might cause a stir, but the deaths of the two bodyguards wouldn't make anyone in Paradise sit up and take notice. The entire town thrived on sensation, but most residents had probably done worse in their day than murder, even to be allowed sanctuary in Paradise. The hotel clerk was a horse of a different color. When he came to, he would tell Plummer's two bodyguards what had happened—and what questions he had been forced to answer.

Slocum considered waiting to see what the two surviving guards did. They might hightail it after their boss to alert him. Or they might not know where he had gone. Plummer was a secretive, sneaky son of a bitch. He had shown that by the way he had married Jane and then left her in the lurch. While some of his men robbed miners at gunpoint, others like Quince went to great lengths to swindle merchants out of their goods. Whatever else George Plummer was, he was a plotter and a planner.

"What's he got in mind for Jane?" Slocum wondered aloud. He closed the corral gate and rode to the end of Paradise's main street before looking out into the distance. Bright starlight outlined the Bitterroot Mountains. Plummer and Jane were somewhere in "the mountains," but Slocum knew firsthand how vast the Bitterroots were.

Had Plummer headed back to Lewiston or even to Orofino? Slocum discounted that as he put his heels to his horse's flanks, cantering toward the dark mountain contours. From all he could tell, Paradise sat in a wide valley surrounded by hills high enough to be difficult to cross. That forced those seeking sanctuary to come through a limited number of passes. But Plummer wouldn't like having to kowtow to guards when he came and went, even if those men worked for him.

Plummer thought of himself as a prince of road agents, and everything he did was intended to set himself apart from the riffraff in his gang.

Faint trails led left and right from the main path, going into the hills. Slocum reckoned those were guarded passages in and out of the valley. What he sought was enough elevation for him to get a good view of the entire countryside.

Slocum pushed his horse to the limit when he saw a likely spot some distance away from the road. He reached the summit, closed his eyes to get them adjusted to the darkness the best he could, then slowly turned, looking out the corners of his eyes. He saw the dust cloud right away. Slocum concentrated on it like a dog going for a bone and studied the lay of the land, trying to make sense of what he saw.

Folks didn't go riding around in the dark, not in this valley, not with Paradise guarded by so many armed men. The only ones he knew who were likely to be out in the countryside were Plummer and Jane. Throwing caution to the winds, Slocum made a beeline for the spot where the dust cloud hung lazily in the night.

By the time he reached the spot, the dust had pretty well been dispersed by a zephyr blowing from the mountains. Slocum turned, until the wind was full in his face, and rode, not looking for spoor. This had to be the way Plummer had gone. If it wasn't, Slocum knew he would never find Jane in time to rescue her from whatever fate her husband had in mind for her.

The thought that Plummer *was* her husband caused Slocum to grind his teeth. She deserved better than a road agent.

By sunup Slocum had found the trail, and he followed it at a quicker pace. But when he smelled a fire ahead and the sharp scent of coffee mingled with the wood smoke, he reined back and rode ahead more slowly. He made certain his six-gun was riding free in his holster and then passed the ring of trees around a large mountain meadow. Not fifty yards off he saw the cook fire blazing merrily, a large coffeepot shoved into it. The brew that would produce would take the paint off a barn. That gave Slocum a hint as to whose camp this was.

As he rode closer, he saw a sapling that danced and bucked about as if it had pulled free of its roots and had developed a hotfoot.

"Jane!" he called. Slocum rode faster and got to the limber tree. Jane was bound and gagged, securely fastened to the sapling's trunk.

"Umgh!" She kicked hard and tried to get her feet under her. They had been tied together, too. The lovely woman was still naked to the waist and her jeans had been almost ripped away. The cool morning air caused gooseflesh to ripple over her sleek, exposed skin.

"Pleased to see you, too," Slocum said. He looked around but saw no one. "Where's your mangy cayuse of a husband?"

She made more choking sounds, but the gag prevented her from giving him any real information. Before he could dismount, a bullet whizzed past his head and put a hole through the brim of his hat. Slocum went for his six-shooter and then froze.

A mountain man had come from the forest, a small deer slung over his broad shoulders. He had fired and now had another round ready to plug Slocum if he moved a muscle.

"You leave my woman alone," the mountain man said in a gravelly voice.

"Yours?" asked Slocum. "How'd that come about?" He ignored Jane's gurgles and grunts.

"I bought her fair and square. If you so much as touch ground, that's where I'll bury you." The mountain man walked forward, keeping the rifle to his shoulder so he could cover Slocum. With a slight shrug, he dumped the deer to the ground. From the way it hit, Slocum reckoned the deer weighed a hundred pounds or more, yet the grizzled man had carried it with no visible effort.

"It's illegal to buy and sell women—or anyone else," Slocum said. "The war settled that."

"Don't care about no War Between the States," the man said. "I bought her. She's mine."

"The man who sold her didn't have the right," Slocum said.

"He tole me he was her husband and had got real tired of her cuz she nagged him to distraction. I paid a fair price," the mountain man said doggedly.

"You know Plummer?"

"We've done business. I supply meat for his shebangs. That's why he thought of me, to reward me for doing such a good job of hunting for him." The man scratched his crotch, then hurriedly reached back to get his finger onto the trigger in case Slocum tried to take advantage of this small flea-bitten distraction.

"She wasn't his to sell," Slocum said.

"Was too," the man insisted. "She's right purty, ain't she?"

"She's mine," Slocum said. He sucked in his breath when he saw the man's finger tighten on the trigger. Getting off another round would solve the mountain man's problems of ownership, but he hesitated. From the way he spoke, Slocum guessed he might have been educated just a little. The veneer of civilization had flaked off during long months alone, but some decency persisted.

"Is not," the man finally declared.

"You got rooked," Slocum said, trying to ignore Jane's frantic, muffled cries of protest. "But I can see you're an honest man and it wouldn't do to take her, though by law that's my right and privilege."

"What are you saying?"

"I'll buy her back, if she hasn't been harmed."

"She didn't come with much in the way of clothes," the man said. "That's why I shot this here deer. It'll make purty doeskin clothes for her. And me and her, well, we ain't had much time. Figgered there'd be plenty of time later for that."

"Glad to hear you're willing to take care of her so well, but she's not yours. What will you take for her? I'll give you what you paid and a little more for your trouble." Slocum saw how Jane's blue eyes flashed angrily.

"I don't know. Nothing like this has happened to me before, not even when I traded for twin sisters. They was Crow and they got away before a full moon came around a second time."

"Take good care of her and I'll trade you enough goods to keep you in style for the winter."

"Winter? It's hardly into summer yet. That'd be a pretty pile of foodstuffs."

"Deal?" asked Slocum.

"When? When you going to trade? She's so purty, I don't know how long I can restrain myself."

Slocum knew a bargaining ploy when he heard one.

"Sundown. That's twelve, fourteen hours off."

"You bring it all up here?" The mountain man scratched himself more vigorously. Slocum guessed the nits were becoming more aggressive as the sun warmed the land and the mountain men walking it.

"Delivered to this very spot, though the going might be tough since that's a steep incline coming up from the valley floor."

"Sundown. And if there ain't enough, deal's off."

"Done," Slocum said, not bothering to look in Jane's direction. He made out enough of the names she called him to speed him on his way. He would be all that and more if he didn't get back with the promised trade goods.

Slocum cut across the valley and approached Paradise from an angle. It had taken all night to reach the mountain man's camp but only a pair of hours to return to the town. Although he kept a sharp eye out, he never saw the outlaw and began to wonder if Plummer had left the valley.

Slocum's life would be simplified if he had. He wasn't sure what to do if he got into Paradise and discovered the outlaw stirring up the town. Better that Plummer was back along the Lewiston-Orofino road plundering and robbing unsuspecting travelers.

But Slocum got to the rear of the saloon without spotting Plummer. This kept him focused on what had to be done. Plummer brought in stolen goods and sold them to merchants in Paradise, probably at an exorbitant price. It wouldn't surprise Slocum to find that Plummer made as much money off supplying the outlaws hiding in town as he did from his other illegal activities, outside the outlaw haven.

Pulling on the reins got his horse turning in a tight circle. As he spun around like a top, Slocum studied the ground behind the saloon and saw the faint tracks left by a heavily laden wagon. Plummer had driven the wagon to the rear door, sold the cases of champagne to the bar owner, then driven off with the rest.

The ruts led across the main street. Slocum ignored the uneasy feeling as he rode in plain sight. It was still early and the residents of Paradise were sleeping off their prior night's debauchery. With any luck, none of Plummer's bodyguards—or the hotel clerk—would notice him.

On the far side of the street he saw more distinct marks in the ground and turned a corner to find a wagon sitting behind the general store. Slocum rode up to the wagon, leaned out of the saddle and stripped back the tarp. A smile split his face. The champagne had been unloaded the night before, but the rest of the supplies were still where Clint Bendix had stored them for transport.

"Hey, what you doin'?" A mousy man poked his head from the door leading into the mercantile.

"I'm doing what Plummer told me to do," Slocum lied. "Where'd you put the mule team that was hitched to this wagon?"

"Out in the stable. Why?"

"Plummer wants the wagon and everything in it moved right away."

"What! He sold me—"

"He sold you squat," Slocum said. "You take it up with the boss. He wanted me to get the wagon and I will, one way or the other."

"Look, I didn't mean anything by it, but I paid a hell of a lot for the food and booze."

Slocum hadn't seen any liquor and wondered if the man

meant the champagne. If so, Plummer had already swindled him.

"Why don't you go get the team and hitch them up for
me," Slocum said, drawing his Colt Navy and laying it
across his thigh. He kept his horse still enough so he could
cover the man, should he take it into his head to be a
hero.

"Mr. Plummer's going to hear it from me," the man
groused, but he lit out for the distant livery. Slocum
heaved a sigh, then waited for the merchant to get the
team hitched up so he could begin the trip back up into
the Bitterroots.

"All that?" the mountain man asked, eyes wide at the
heavily laden wagon.

"That's what I promised. You didn't touch her, did
you?"

"What if I did?"

"No whiskey," Slocum said.

"You got likker in there?" The mountain man licked
his dried lips, signaling his immense thirst.

"Take a look," Slocum said. He had pawed through the
cargo on his way up the winding mountain trail and had
found an entire case of pure grain alcohol. A barkeep
would cut that five- or ten-to-one with molasses for color,
water, a pinch of gunpowder and nitric acid for kick, and
would make a fortune. Drunk straight, it could send a man
on a bender that wouldn't end for a month.

"Mister, put 'er there," the mountain man said, shoving
out his filthy paw of a hand. Slocum shook, waiting to
see if the man might try to double-cross him.

Before coming into camp, Slocum had spied awhile and
satisfied himself that Jane was still tied up, half-naked and
madder than ever. Other than this, she didn't look any the
worse for wear and tear, leading him to believe the mountain man was keeping his side of the bargain.

"I'll go fetch my property," Slocum said. But he spoke to the man's broad back. The mountain man dug through the cans of ham to get to the pure alcohol.

Slocum wanted to be far, far away when the mountain man got roaring drunk.

He walked around the wagon to the sapling. Jane had almost pulled its roots out of the ground from her struggles. She glared at him, her naked breasts thrust out defiantly, as if daring him to make a comment.

Slocum drew his knife and cut the ropes around her ankles, then her wrists. She ripped out the gag, but before she could launch into a tirade, Slocum clamped his hand over her mouth.

"Save it," he said, inclining his head in the direction of the mountain man, who now sat in the back of the wagon, guzzling the alcohol. A shot would knock a normal man on his ass. A quarter of the bottle had already vanished down the man's gullet.

"Oh, oh, oh," sputtered an enraged Jane, but she let him help her to her feet. She was wobbly since the ropes had cut off circulation in her feet. Slocum put his arm around her and helped her to his horse. He wished he had remembered to bring a second mount, but he had been too intent on stealing the wagon filled with supplies.

"Bendix doesn't need to know what happened to one of his wagons, but it went for a good cause."

"Good? Why, how can you say paying ransom to that . . . that . . ." Jane began to sputter again. Slocum got the horse walking away from camp, to put as much distance between them and the mountain man as he could. All hell would be breaking loose—in Paradise, here, throughout the Bitterroots—when Plummer found that all his plans were unraveling.

Slocum couldn't wait for the final blow-off.

17

"Getting away from Paradise isn't going to be easy," Slocum said.

"You should have killed him."

"I didn't have the chance," Slocum said. "I never saw Plummer when he wasn't surrounded by bodyguards."

"George? I didn't mean him. I meant that terrible, smelly man back there. The one you *traded* me for all those supplies."

"He didn't do anything wrong," Slocum said, surprised at the woman's vehemence. "He works for Plummer as a hunter. He shoots deer and bear for meat."

"He smells like a bear," Jane said hotly. "He *bought* me and you went along with it. You should have plugged him smack between the eyes."

"Why bother with the man doing the buying? Why not be mad at your husband?"

"George is a snake in the grass and that's his nature. He wanted to torment me and that's how he chose to do it."

Slocum started to ask what had happened to her back at the hotel, but he held his question. Ahead he saw dark shadows moving along the trail. He veered off at an angle and sat, waiting. Jane saw the riders, also, and fell silent, but Slocum knew she was still stewing about her ill treatment.

The knot of four men passed by without knowing they were within miles of anyone else. Slocum waited a decent interval before getting back onto the trail.

"Outlaws," he said. "We're going to have to be careful."

"John, can we rest a spell? I'm feeling a bit woozy after all that's been done to me."

Slocum went deeper into the thicket, until he found a small ring of trees that would shield them from all but the most diligent search. As far as he knew, no one hunted them. The mountain man was happy with his grain alcohol and had probably passed out by now. Unless the hotel clerk convinced Plummer that there was real trouble brewing, the leader of the road agents wasn't likely to send out scouts. Plummer was in a position to think that everything was going smooth as silk, all his problems solved after he gave Jane to the hunter.

"We can camp here for a while. It's a good thing I rummaged through the cargo in that wagon and got some food." Jane slid off the horse and wrapped her arms around herself. Slocum followed to the ground and took the saddlebags off and handed them to her. "Find something to fix for us."

"What am I? Your slave?"

Slocum laughed and went to scout the area to be sure they were truly alone. He hadn't gone ten paces when he heard Jane's delighted cry. By the time he returned, he saw she had on the fresh man's shirt he had found in the cargo and had set aside, knowing she would need it.

"I couldn't find any jeans that I thought would fit. But a shirt's easy to come by."

"John, you're a prince!" She threw her arms around his neck and kissed him firmly.

"Aren't you hungry?" he asked.

She moved back a few inches and looked up at him. Her blue eyes twinkled and a smile curled her lips enough to bring out dimples.

"I am—for you."

She kissed him passionately again. Slocum found himself getting aroused in a hurry by the way her tongue probed his mouth, then retreated to allow his to surge out. He broke off the kiss to move back along the line of her jaw, kissing as he went, until he came to her delicate earlobe. He caught the tender flesh between his teeth and nibbled enough to make her tense. She gasped with desire every time he bit down.

"Yes, John," she whispered hotly. "That's what I want. And more. I want more!"

Her fingers pressed into his chest, fumbling in haste to unbutton his shirt. She ripped it open and stroked through the mat of hair she found. Then Jane's nimble fingers worked lower. Standing on tiptoe, she repositioned herself so she could thrust her hand down between his jeans and belly and plunge low enough to tease his rising manhood.

"That's awkward," he said. "Let me help you." He unfastened his gun belt and let it drop, but Jane was already working on the buttons holding his jeans together. Slocum let out a gasp when she found his rigid organ and grabbed hold of it.

"That's paradise," she corrected. Jane dropped to her knees and buried her face in his groin. He felt her demanding lips wetly circle his rigid shaft and then take him into her mouth. The tongue that had delighted him before, aroused him completely now.

He reached down and ran his fingers through her long, dark hair, then slipped his hands under the shirt he had brought for her and stripped it off. Her snowy white flesh slowly revealed itself to him, shoulders first and then the twin mounds of her firm, perky breasts.

As pleasurable as her lips and tongue were on him, Slocum wanted more. He lifted her away from her post and kissed her fully on the lips again. As he did, his hands cupped her breasts, then squeezed down. This brought squeals of desire from Jane.

"Pinch them. Pinch the nipples, John," she said. When he did, a shudder passed from head to toe and back, robbing her of strength in her legs. She began to sag. He followed her down.

"That was so nice," she said, her eyes half-hooded now. As Jane lay back on the ground, she lifted her rump and began working to unfasten her jeans. They came off quickly, almost in tatters.

Slocum looked from her trembling white slopes down across her belly to the dark-furred triangle between her thighs. He ran his finger from one ruddy, hard nipple down the slope of the fleshy cone, across her heaving belly and into the tangled fleecy jungle. His finger curled about and slipped into her steamy interior. She was moist and ready for him.

He put his hands on the woman's strong thighs and parted them until she was wantonly wide open for him.

"Hurry, John. I'm burning up inside. I need you so!"

He felt the same way. His iron-hard shaft throbbed with need, but Slocum wasn't going to hurry. There was no reason not to enjoy one another as long as possible. He positioned himself, bent forward and let her take him in hand again so she could guide him in.

The purpled knob atop his organ touched the wet nether lips, parted them and began slowly entering territory both known and mysterious. He felt her quake around him as he sank ever deeper. Then there was nowhere else to go. He felt her entirely around, clutching fiercely.

"Move, John, move damn you! I can't stand this! You're driving me wild!"

He didn't obey. He swallowed hard as he fought to

control himself. She tried to milk him with her powerful
inner grip. When he was enough in command of his rampaging feelings, he started rotating his hips. He stirred his
fleshy rod around within her like a spoon in a mixing
bowl.

Jane began thrashing about, moaning and sobbing and
begging him for more.

He slowly retreated, until only the tip of his column
remained within her. Then he rushed forward. Heat from
his passage spread like wildfire throughout their loins,
turning into a raging forest fire that consumed them.

Jane lifted her behind off the ground and tried to shove
herself down as hard into him as he was stroking forward.
The carnal friction triggered another climax in the
woman's tender body and almost caused Slocum to lose
control. But he kept moving, grinding his crotch into hers,
building the tensions until the very sky exploded.

The heat deep inside him reached the point of no return.
Slocum began to melt, then he exploded like a stick of
dynamite. By this time Jane was clawing at his arms and
hunching up to get even more of his meaty spike deep
into her molten core.

Together, they rocked through total release, until they
lay exhausted on the forest floor.

"I never thought it could be so . . . ," she began.

"Good?" he suggested.

"Intense. So incredibly intense. Good doesn't come
close to describing what I felt." Jane rolled onto her side
and rested her cheek on his chest.

Slocum lay on his back staring up into the leafy forest
cover. For the first time in months he felt content, com-
fortable, at peace with the world. He slipped off to sleep.

He came awake at the sound of something moving
nearby. His hand went for his six-shooter, but he found
only bare skin. Slocum rolled, got his gun and came up
onto his knees.

"Aren't you a sight," said Jane, laughing. "A mighty fine one, I admit, but still a sight."

Slocum saw that the dark-haired woman had rifled through the saddlebags and found the provisions he had packed. The meal she fixed was simple but adequate to fill the void in his belly.

He stuck his six-shooter back into the holster and began dressing.

"Thanks for getting the food," he said.

"You brought it. What are we going to do now?"

"Eat," Slocum said.

"No, no, John. That's not what I meant, and you know it. We're stuck in Paradise, every man with a gun is aiming at us, and getting out could be a real chore. A dangerous one."

Slocum gnawed on a piece of the jerky and eyed the can of tomatoes sitting on the ground where she had put it.

"So?" she demanded when he didn't answer right away.

"We get back to Lewiston, tell Sheriff Allen about this place, then let the law do the dirty work."

"I want him. I want to feel his throat under my fingers," she said heatedly. "If I can't kill him then I want to divorce him."

"How about a divorce and seeing him sent to prison? There's a mighty nasty prison in Boise."

"That would do," she said, cooling down a mite. "As long as he doesn't get away with treating me the way he did."

"George Plummer's got a lot to answer for," Slocum said, his mind turning over the possibilities. "First, he has to get us out of here."

Jane looked at him curiously, waiting for him to explain.

• • •

"How did you know he'd be driving a wagon out of town?" Jane asked in a low voice. They crouched down and walked toward the back of a storage shed where another of Clint Bendix's wagons was parked. A team of mules had been hitched but the wagon was empty.

"After I stole the one he'd sold to the owner of the general store, I reckoned he had to replace the goods. Plummer makes a fortune selling to the people of Paradise. If he doesn't bring them enough to keep them in style, they'll decide it's time to move on. Why ruin such a sweet deal?"

"So he swindles some other packer out of his cargo?"

"Right," Slocum said, lifting the tarp tossed into the bed of the wagon. He looked around, then motioned for Jane to crawl under. He quickly joined her.

"This could be fun," she said, snuggling closer to him.

"It won't be in a while," Slocum predicted. He shoved his rifle into a groove in the side of the wagon so it wouldn't rattle around, then lay back, trying to cushion himself the best he could.

"I could stay like this, oh, forever," she said.

Ten minutes later the driver and three other outlaws came up, half-drunk and boisterous. When the brake came off the wheel, the wagon lurched and threw Slocum and Jane around. Then the going got rough.

"Does he have to hit every pothole and rock in the road?" she complained after a few minutes.

"Quiet," Slocum said. "Remember. You thought this was fun."

He had to endure her stony silence for another few miles, but that suited him fine. Now and then he peeked out from under the tarp. The riders flanked the wagon and the driver sang at the top of his lungs. But this served as a warning when the man suddenly fell silent.

Slocum moved the tarp back and squinted into the bright sun. He guessed it was close to noon from the heat building up under the canvas. The driver and the men riding alongside all stopped and simply waited.

"What's wrong?" whispered Jane.

"We're close to the pass leading out of the valley," Slocum said. He couldn't make head nor tail of their location, but this was the only logical reason they'd stop and simply sit, waiting for something to happen.

"Where'd that lazy galoot get off to?" grumbled the driver.

"Off takin' a leak, maybe. The boss'll cut it off if he finds he left his post for very long."

"He done worse'n that to the Baltimore Kid. He staked him out in the sun till he died. Couldn't ever tell if it was from the sun or the ants chewin' away at his flesh."

"At least he never left his post again, not like this yahoo. Where did he get off to?" complained the driver. "Wait, there he is. Over in the trees. He's supposed to be up in the rocks where he can cover the pass."

"Hey, Vince," shouted a rider. "We got to get this here wagon over to Quince's shebang."

"How many of you is there?" came back the weak question.

Slocum chanced another glance in the guard's direction. From the look of the man he had spent the night puking out his guts. He was whiter than a sheet and his hands shook when he held his rifle. Now and again, he made a tiny retching noise and turned to one side. Slocum heaved a sigh. If he had known the guard was going to be so ill disposed, he could have ridden right past him and not had to leave his horse and saddle behind outside Paradise.

"Ten thousand," shouted the driver. "And we got ten thousand more in the back of my wagon."

"Get the hell out of here," groaned the guard. "I feel like I'm fixin' to die and don't need your lip."

The wagon jerked suddenly as the team began pulling. Slocum settled back and let the noise of the wheels clattering around the rocky pass cover his voice.

"We'll be on the other side soon enough," he said. "Wait for a chance to slip out. You first, then I'll follow."

"What if they see me?" Jane asked anxiously.

"Then I have to kill them."

"Why not just shoot them now?" she asked. "You could get two or three of them before the others noticed. Give me the rifle and I'll take out a pair of them and you can have the rest."

"You're getting more bloodthirsty by the day," Slocum said.

"It comes from being so close to George Garson— Plummer, I mean," she said.

"No gunplay unless it's necessary. I've got a plan and it works better if they all reach Quince's place without knowing we were even here."

"All right," Jane said dubiously.

An hour later the road changed again, from solid rock to occasional dirt. Then the easier ride signaled they were rolling on hard-packed earth with only occasional rocks in the roadway. Slocum gripped the woman's arm and indicated she ought to get ready to jump off.

He pulled his rifle free from its tight berth, moved away a bit of the canvas and saw the riders coursing ahead of the wagon.

"Go!" he said.

Jane never hesitated. She wiggled about, then flopped awkwardly out of the wagon. Slocum thought he heard her land butt-first in the road, but the clank of chains and the braying of the mules as they strained to pull the wagon up an incline covered any small noise. He checked again, and saw that the outriders were scouting on the far side of the hill and that the driver concentrated totally on keeping his team moving.

With curses and cracks from the long bullwhip, the driver guided the mules expertly enough.

Slocum slid on his belly out of the wagon bed, caught at the rear and did a somersault, landing hard in the road. He twisted around onto his belly, rifle pointed in the direction of the wagon as it topped the hill. Then all that remained was a dust cloud marking the wagon's presence.

Standing, he brushed himself off and went to find Jane. They had quite a walk into Lewiston ahead of them.

18

"This is mighty risky," Clint Bendix said. He scratched his chin and then leaned back in the chair so that the front legs left the floor and he propped himself against the wall. "Expensive, too. Ain't sure I got the money to risk on such a chancy plan, Slocum."

"You probably won't get any of the goods in the six wagons back." Slocum had explained how they had escaped Paradise and all he had seen. He had refrained from telling his friend that the champagne was powerful tasty. Bendix had suffered the death of a thousand cuts hearing how his merchandise had been swindled and then sold to outlaws in a town hidden away in the Bitterroot Mountains.

"Why'd I want to go and do such a damn fool thing, then?" Bendix asked.

"The reward might be enough to help pay for new wagons," Jane said. "For an entire gang the size of Plummer's, you could rake in a considerable sum of money."

"I need to pay for the *old* ones. Hell, I needed the sale of all that fancy ass stuff to pay for the merchandise and wages. You're still not gettin' paid, Slocum, not till I get my full amount back. I got creditors breathin' down my neck wantin' their money 'fore I do anything else."

Slocum doubted that. Clint Bendix had run a successful freight company for too many years. While he might have borrowed the money to buy the goods, Slocum doubted that, too. Bendix might be flat broke, but he wasn't in debt.

"Then consider the public good you'll be doing," Jane went on. "You'll be a hero to every mule skinner who ever got robbed along that road. Your name'll be mentioned in stories of heroes told around campfires."

"You think so?"

Slocum was surprised that the notion of being a legend appealed so to Bendix. He had thought the man driven only by money, but this was a new side and one Jane had immediately spotted.

"Definitely," she said.

"Might be I can get a wagon or two scared up," Bendix said. "But I'll want the sheriff to have enough deputies so I don't get my damn fool head blowed off."

"Where is Sheriff Allen?" Jane asked.

Slocum had hunted for the lawman after they had hoofed it into Lewiston, but as best he could tell the sheriff was out serving process. This was one of the few moneymaking jobs a lawman could take. Allen had mentioned a family, and living off what Nez Perce County paid him would be nigh on impossible. The extra money from court proceedings and delivering legal papers would keep his family from starving.

And it was nowhere as dangerous as riding after the likes of George Plummer and his gang. As much as Allen might talk about the hefty reward offered for the road agents, he was no man's fool. It was easier and safer handing someone a court summons.

"Don't matter where the sheriff is. The sight of a badge'd only scare off a chickenshit like George Plum-

mer," Bendix said. "Let me go talk to a few folks and see
what I can rustle up. I know I can get two wagons. And
that good-for-nothing at the livery has a small wagon I
might use to make a caravan look more impressive.
Then . . ." Clint Bendix wandered off muttering to himself
about what he could do.

"You talked him into it. Thanks," Slocum said.

"No need to thank me. I'm as eager to see George
Plummer behind bars as you are. More. But I've got to
find a lawyer and get new divorce papers drawn up.
George took the set I brought from Nebraska, tore them
up and threw them in my face."

"What else did he do?" Slocum remembered too well
the rumpled bed in the Paradise hotel. From the pinched
look on Jane's face he guessed what else had happened.

"Enough to make me want to be rid of him forever.
But I want a divorce before he swings from a gallows. It
would be so humiliating to have my husband executed."

"Not your fault," Slocum said.

"Marrying him was," Jane said, color coming back to
her cheeks. "I heard tell there's a new lawyer in town. I
should go talk with him. Will you come along, John?"

"I've got a few chores of my own to tend to," Slocum
said. "I'll meet you at the Trail's End Café for supper
around seven."

"Very well." Jane hesitated, looked around to see if
anyone was looking, then hastily kissed him. She smiled,
dimples showing, then rushed off like a schoolgirl.

Slocum perched on the hitching rail along the boardwalk for a moment, watching her go. She was a mighty
fine-looking woman, but he was beginning to think she
harbored notions about him that would never come true.
He heaved himself off the rough rail and went to the Lewiston jail to ask when the sheriff would return. For Slocum's plan to work, he needed a considerable amount of
firepower—and he wanted to tell Allen about the outlaw

town up in the mountains. For the sheriff to tackle that many road agents would require an Army company or two.

From what he had seen and heard in Paradise, Slocum knew the sheriff would have no trouble convincing the cavalry detachment to join the manhunt.

He poked his head into the jail and saw a deputy nodding off in the noonday heat. The deputy stirred, then snorted and came awake. His hand reached for the shotgun on the desk, and then he settled down when he saw who interrupted his siesta.

"What you need, Mr. Slocum?"

"I checked this morning and nobody knew when the sheriff would be back. Any news?"

"Nary a whisper. When he left he said he might be gone a couple days but not past the end of the week."

"How are your prisoners holding up?" Slocum saw Luke Latham in the nearest cell. The outlaw glared at him, but Slocum had an uneasy feeling about Latham's demeanor. Something struck him as wrong. He hastily looked into the next cell, where the other two outlaws sat with their heads together, whispering their plans.

"I wish the judge'd get here so we can hang 'em all."

"That wasn't the deal the sheriff made," Slocum pointed out.

"Just my opinion. If what they say brings in Plummer, might be they deserve to ride out of Lewiston free men. Me, I'd be happy to cut 'em in half with a scattergun." He reached over to the desk and pressed his hand into the wood stock of the shotgun.

"I'll come back around sunset to see if the sheriff's back," Slocum said.

He stepped into the street, the uneasy feeling growing. He shielded his eyes against the bright Idaho sun as he looked up and down the main street. He couldn't help comparing this with Paradise. Lewiston was a poor country cousin when it came to the nicer things like gaslights and well-built stores. But Slocum would trade a dozen towns like Paradise for the honest people of Lewiston any day.

He shrugged and thought he was beginning to jump at ghosts when he heard a horse galloping in the distance. Stepping out into the street, he saw a rider coming hell-bent for leather. The rider whooped and hollered and kicked up more than his share of dust. As the horse and rider drew closer, Slocum saw the rope wrapped around the saddle horn and someone being dragged along behind.

"Stop!" shouted Slocum. He ran toward the rider, who reined back. A cloud of dust momentarily obscured the man as horse hooves dug deep into the street.

Choking, Slocum made his way through the thick cloud and got out his Colt Navy. He had it cocked and aimed at the rider when he saw who had been dragged behind.

"Sheriff!"

The rider let out another whoop and started firing at Slocum. The first two bullets missed. Slocum never gave the gunman a third shot. He lifted his six-gun and pulled back smoothly on the trigger. The gun bucked and roared, sending the rider tumbling from the saddle. This spooked his horse. Slocum continued to act instinctively.

He ran alongside the horse a few paces, before it could get up much speed, and vaulted into the saddle. Bending over, he reached down and caught at the reins. He missed repeatedly and knew he had to try something else fast. From his position hanging around the horse's neck, feet unable to find the swinging, bouncing stirrups, he wrestled the horse to a halt. After the frightened, lathered animal stopped its running, Slocum struggled to unfasten the rope from the pommel.

"Sheriff, are you all right?" Slocum asked, dropping from the horse to see to the lawman's condition.

"Been better," Sheriff Allen said. He sat up, looking

the worse for wear. His chest was scratched and bloody and his hands were rope-burned. If he had put his face next to a plate of hamburger, only his best friends would have been able to tell the difference. But the sheriff was alive and getting madder by the second.

"That son of a bitch! I'll see a noose around his neck!"

"I shot him," Slocum said. "Who was he?"

"Not him. He's nothing," Allen said, spitting in the dead rider's direction. "George Plummer ordered this done. I was out serving a subpoena when I was hit from behind. Plummer ordered me all trussed up and they brought me within a quarter mile of town. Then Plummer left."

"He left? He didn't stay to see the fun?" Slocum asked. The uneasy feeling returned.

"Ten minutes after he left, this sidewinder started me running, then dragged me the rest of the way into town."

"If he'd wanted you dead, he could have shot you in the back," Slocum said.

"What do you mean, Slocum?"

"The jailhouse!" Slocum spun and tried to get a good look back down the street, but the dust cloud hung in the air, obscuring his vision. "He's going to break out Latham and the other two."

"Son of a bitch!" Allen cried. The sheriff went to the dead outlaw, pried the six-shooter from the man's hand and hobbled through the dust toward the jail. By now a considerable crowd had gathered.

"Get your guns," Allen called to the crowd. "Plummer's bustin' out his henchmen!"

Slocum and Allen got through the dusty patch and saw that more than a jailbreak was in progress. Orange flames licked at the sides of the jail, coming from inside and roaring skyward.

"He set fire to the jail. Ring the alarm!" shouted Slocum. "Get the volunteers out to fight the fire."

The disaster feared most by sensible townspeople in the West was fire. And George Plummer had torched the jail and two buildings next to it. If they didn't put out the fire quickly, the entire town of Lewiston would go up in smoke.

19

"Fire!"

The dread cry spread through Lewiston as fast as the fire itself. Men and women poured from the buildings and began forming bucket brigades. Slocum tried to get into the jailhouse to see if the deputy had escaped. The heat drove him back.

"You're gonna set yourself on fire," Bendix said, coming up. "Ain't nuthin' in there worth savin'."

"Might be the deputy," Slocum said. He grabbed a saddle blanket and doused it in the water trough, then slung it over his head.

"Slocum, don't!" shouted Clint Bendix, but Slocum ignored him and plunged into the inferno. Heat hit him like a fist. Every ache and pain and injury he had accumulated since coming to Idaho Territory pained him something fierce. Every breath he took was of superheated air that seared his lungs, but Slocum wasn't going to give up.

He crashed through the burning rubble and got to the desk where the deputy had been seated. He saw the body on the floor and knew right away the man was dead. The side of his face had been shot off before the fire had been started.

As if reinforcing his danger, the deputy's shotgun discharged. The shells in the cabinet across the office began firing, too. The heat had dried out most of the water from Slocum's protecting blanket, but he still had one more place to look. Doubled over, he fought his way back to the jail cells. The door of the first one, where Luke Latham had been, stood wide open. The other cell with his two cohorts remained closed.

Slocum jerked away when he inadvertently touched an iron bar, already too hot for comfort. He backed out, then tumbled into the street, where Sheriff Allen and Clint Bendix doused him with water.

"You were on fire, Slocum," accused Bendix. "Don't you know better than to leave it where it is?"

"Sorry," Slocum said. He looked up at the sheriff. "Your deputy's dead. Plummer shot him and then started the fire."

"There's something more, isn't there?" Allen said. He looked like a parody of a human being. The cuts on his face still oozed blood into the dust he'd picked up while being dragged, but the soot and spots where blistering had started told Slocum he had tried to follow him into the jailhouse.

"Can't tell if Plummer plugged the other two prisoners or just doused them with coal oil and then set fire to them and the jail. Both are dead, too."

"They turned on Latham," Allen said. "They were murdering pigs, but they deserved better."

"They deserved nooses around their necks. You was lettin' 'em off too easy," flared Clint Bendix. "They're all road agents, swindlers, stone killers!"

Slocum beat out the final spots on the saddle blanket that had ignited. He stood.

"We can argue about it later. Plummer took his revenge on them for being turncoats. Don't forget them. Those are more murders for the judge to rule on."

"We've got to catch the bastard first," said Sheriff Allen.

"First we have to put out the fire," Slocum said. The heat from the blaze that had now consumed the four buildings nearest the jail drove them back down the street to a spot where it was tolerable, barely.

They joined a bucket brigade, passing buckets filled at a water trough, down the length of the street so the man closest could throw what remained in the bucket onto the voracious fire. Slocum knew they might as well be pissing on the flames for all the good it did, but they had to try.

"Up there, Slocum. Up on the second floor of the hotel," shouted the sheriff over the roar of the fire. "I see a woman in a window."

"Ain't nobody gonna go into that," Clint Bendix said, already dousing himself in water. Slocum and the sheriff followed him into the water trough and dripped as they raced for the hotel's front porch. Bendix kicked in the door and let out a blast of flame. Both Slocum and Sheriff Allen waited for it to suck back into the lobby, then plunged inside.

"The stairs! Looks like they might go at any second."

"Got to try," Slocum said. He grabbed a straight-backed chair and tossed it onto the smoldering staircase. He jumped onto the chair and felt the stairs beneath crumbling and then giving way entirely. Slocum found himself balancing on the chair back as it stretched over a span of three crumbling risers. He made a frantic leap and got to the top of the steps before they collapsed under him.

Falling to his belly, he wiggled like a snake down the hall, trying to figure out which room the woman had been trapped inside. Slocum found it hard to keep his bearings. The smoke made his eyes water and the fumes caused him to choke and cough.

"Where are you?" he called. "I need to know where you are!"

He heard faint rustling sounds. It might have been from the fire devouring curtains or it could have been something else. Slocum had no time left. He felt the skin on his back tingling from the heat. He crawled to the door that was his best guess to hide the woman, spun around and then kicked with his feet. Again. Another time and then the door fell inward, knocked off its hinges.

A quick glance showed him why he had been able to kick in the door. The doorjamb had partly burned through.

He saw the woman collapsed by the window. On hands and knees, Slocum hurried to her side and lifted her chin. Her eyelids fluttered, showing she was still alive.

He gathered her in his arms, got his feet under him and heaved to a standing position. The floor began sagging, weakened by the flames. Slocum turned to the window and leaned out.

"Catch her! Somebody catch her!" He didn't wait to see if anyone was below or had even heard his cry for help. Slocum tossed the woman out blindly because the smoke had robbed him of sight. He staggered as the floor broke under him.

Sharp planking tore at his boot, holding him like a wolf caught in a steel-toothed trap. Slocum jerked frantically, then calmed down. He couldn't see and was caught, but if he panicked he would also be dead. Working by feel, he pried loose the board holding his foot, then reached out, found the window frame and dived through it.

Instinct took over. He somersaulted around and got his feet under him before he landed. The impact sent him reeling as he fell headlong to the ground. But he was out of the burning building—alive.

"We got her, Slocum," came Bendix's voice. "You're 'bout the dumbest son of a buck I ever did see, but you saved her."

"Yeah, you saved her," came the sheriff's voice. "Now let's get back to the bucket brigade."

Slocum sat up, then recoiled when a bucket of water struck him full in the face. He sputtered, then caught another one. His eyes burned like the very fire, but his vision returned as he got the smoke and ash out.

"We got a big chore ahead of us," Sheriff Allen said in a softer tone. "You up to it?"

"Of course I am," Slocum said. And he was, working past exhaustion with the rest of the citizens of Lewiston.

Men drove endlessly from the river bringing water into the troughs so the others fighting the fire had something to fling. Now and again, after they had toiled away for almost an hour, the men in the line began to stumble and fail. Jane and other women tended them the best they could, but in the end, the fire burned itself out by devouring all fuel not denied it by the struggling men and their bucket brigade.

Half of Lewiston had been lost, but the townspeople still cheered. They had saved the other half.

Sooty and sapped of all strength, Slocum flopped on the steps of the saloon. There was some mercy in the world, and it didn't come only from leaving a watering hole intact for the thirsty firemen. If the fire had reached this structure, it would have gone up in a huge explosion. The back room was stacked with barrels of trade whiskey and all the filth that got poured into the bottles to give the booze flavor and kick.

"How much gunpowder do you have back there?" Slocum asked the barkeep.

"Couple kegs." The barkeep whistled. "Never thought on it till you mentioned it. That would have taken out the other half of town, wouldn't it?"

"With all the whiskey pouring onto the floor as the kegs broke open, it would have been like throwing dried firewood into hellfire," Slocum said. "Why don't you open the spigots and give the men who saved your hide and business free beer?"

"Beer, hell! I'll give 'em the good stuff." The barkeep went into the middle of the street, cupped his hands around his mouth and shouted in a stentorian voice, "Whiskey's on the house. Better hurry 'cuz you won't hear me make this offer a second time!"

A cheer went up as the men rushed for the saloon.

Slocum barely got out of the way of the stampede. He sank down at the edge of the boardwalk, idly snuffed out a smoldering ember that had flown from down the street, and leaned back. Exhaustion ought to have seized him like a fist now, but he felt a fire burning inside worse than that which had devoured half of Lewiston.

"I feel the same way," came a soft voice.

"How do you know how I'm feeling?" Slocum asked Jane.

"I can read your face like a book. You want George as badly as I do. We might have different reasons but the end is the same."

"You did good work back there, helping the men who flagged."

"You were brave, John, running into the jail the way you did. Brave but foolish."

Slocum couldn't have left the deputy inside if he had been alive. He wasn't even sure he could have left the two owlhoots in the cell. Plummer had saved him that added aggravation by killing them both.

"Did Bendix get his wagons moved in time? He had them down the street near the livery." Slocum had watched the haystacks behind the stables go up as fast as if they had been doused in kerosene. Some horses had been burned inside, but the ostler had gotten most far enough away so they wouldn't try running back into the blaze.

"He's got four wagons. All of them are down by the river."

"Good." Slocum leaned back and closed his eyes. Grit

and ash caused tears to form. He hastily wiped them away
and blinked furiously a few times to get the rest of the
cinders out.

"I saved my papers, too," Jane said. She rummaged in
a voluminous pocket on the skirt she wore and pulled out
a sheaf of papers. "The lawyer drew these up before the
fire. See? All I need do is get George to sign here. There
is some legal problem, however."

"What's that?"

"What name does he sign? Garson? Plummer?"

"Make him sign both, to be on the safe side," Slocum
said. "In blood."

"That'll come later, John," she said. "I feel as if this is
all my fault. I've put you through so much."

"You didn't make Plummer steal Bendix's merchandise. You didn't make Plummer a crook. He was that way
when he married you. You're just one of his victims."

"I don't like being a victim," she said.

"Neither do I." Slocum got to his feet, then reached out
a filthy hand to help Jane to her feet. "Let's find Bendix
and the sheriff. We've got plans to make and a crook to
catch."

20

"You really think they're gonna buy this, Slocum?" asked Clint Bendix. He scratched himself as he stared across the roadway at the five battered wagons lined up on the outskirts of Lewiston. "The whole danged town's recoverin' from the fire. Why would any fool want to move their goods to Orofino instead of sellin' 'em here? Ever'one knows how much is needed to rebuild a place that's been burned to the ground."

"Money," Slocum said confidently. "I had the sheriff spread the rumor that the money in the bank was all burned up and that everyone's flat broke because of it."

"Fire didn't come close to the bank," Bendix said. He frowned as he stared at Slocum.

"We know that, but the talk is that the heat turned all the greenbacks in the vault to ash, and the banker isn't honoring anyone's claim for gold bullion stored there fearing he'd have a run on his bank like the one in '73."

"Sounds mighty flimsy," Bendix said, putting his new hat back on his shaggy head.

"Looks good, though," Slocum said as he nudged Bendix in the ribs to quiet him. Two men sauntered up to the rear wagon, trying to seem as if they weren't interested in the contents. They exchanged a few hasty words, then obviously came to a mutual agreement. While one stood watch, the other untied a few ropes and dived under the canvas covering, burrowing about like a badger.

"Reckon he's takin' the bait?" asked Bendix in a low voice.

"He'll never bother opening any of the crates," Slocum said. "He's too intent on taking an inventory of what he *thinks* is in the boxes."

"There he goes to the next wagon," Bendix said, his tone turning more cheerful. "We got them dead to rights!"

"Don't spook them," Slocum warned. They stood in the shade a dozen yards away, watching as the two outlaws systematically worked to record everything in the wagons. It took them the better part of twenty minutes, and Slocum decided they were working too slow. If the outlaws thought this was too easy, they might get suspicious.

Slocum pointed, waited for his friend's response, then he and Bendix stepped out into the bright sunlight, talking as if they had been down the street drinking at the saloon. Slocum was careful not to look directly at the man still rooting around in the fifth wagon. The other one hissed to his partner, and the two had vamoosed by the time Slocum and Bendix reached the lead wagon.

"Think they'll stick around and watch what we do?"

"I doubt it," Slocum said, "but I'll do some scouting to be certain." His plan required complete surprise. If Plummer got wind of a trap, he would make himself scarce and the sheriff might never run him down.

Slocum mounted and rode slowly in the direction taken by the two road agents. A smile curled his lips when he saw the dust cloud left behind as the two raced out of Lewiston, on their way to Quince's shebang. He took nothing for granted as he continued to patrol until he was certain that Plummer hadn't left any of his gang around to spy on the wagons. He was glad to see that Plummer was as confident as ever. The leader of the road agents had a swindle that had worked before, and he obviously saw no reason to jeopardize the way it operated now.

Slocum got back to the wagons and found Clint Bendix already in the driver's box of the lead wagon.

"You staying up front of the caravan?" Slocum asked. "That's likely to be the most dangerous place if anything goes wrong."

"You mean Plummer might take it into his head to kill the lead driver, stop the wagon train, then just steal ever'thin' at gunpoint?" Bendix bit off a plug of tobacco and began chewing. When he got enough juice in his mouth, he spat. The wet brown gob arched up, caught a fleck of passing sunlight and then smashed into a rock beside the road, showing his contempt for Plummer and the danger he posed.

"Something like that," Slocum said. "You still game?"

"Feelin' game 'n' I smell gamy," Clint Bendix said, smiling. "The rest of them greenhorn mule skinners ready to drive the wagons?"

Slocum rode the length of the wagon train and then back to Bendix. The drivers appeared apprehensive, but determined. This was good enough for Slocum.

"Roll 'em!" he called, lifting his arm high to get everyone's attention, then pointing in the direction of Quince's shebang.

"Yee-haw!" shouted Bendix, snapping his long whip to get the mules pulling. Wood creaked, leather harness moaned and chains clanked as the powerful teams strained to haul the heavy wagons. Slocum rode to the rear of the wagons again and then watched as they vanished out of Lewiston. It wasn't his place to ride guard alongside the wagons this time, as much as he itched to. When they rattled into Quince's shebang, there couldn't be a hint of trouble or the outlaw would simply chase them off.

But Slocum wished he could be riding along with his

friend, up at the front where the danger would be the greatest.

"You can't," Jane Garson said, coming up beside him. She sat astride a roan mare that stepped lively and gave her more than enough trouble to keep under control. The horses left in Lewiston after the fire had reduced the choices available, but Slocum saw she was a good enough horsewoman to show the animal who was boss. Still, Jane had to be vigilant to keep the horse from bolting.

"You a mind reader now?" he asked, grinning.

"I don't have to be," Jane said. "I feel the same way. What are we supposed to do? Wait for the shooting to start, then ride in?"

"Nope," Slocum said. "We wait for the shooting to stop, then we ride in."

"Killjoy," she said, pouting prettily. "Let's go, John. I've got the divorce papers in my saddlebags, and I want to buttonhole that son of a bitch before he weasels free again. If the sheriff locks him up, I might not even be allowed to talk to him."

"He won't get away," Slocum said. He started at a steady walk, but Jane's horse almost ran away with her. Slocum considered offering to trade but knew she wasn't in any mood to permit it. She was apprehensive and anxious to be finished with George Plummer, and any hint of criticism would only irritate her.

Slocum caught up with Jane and pointed to a side road.

"That curves around through the countryside and comes out by the creek near Quince's shebang. We can wait there until the excitement's over, then go on up to the roadhouse after the sheriff is finished."

"You make it sound so easy, John," Jane said worriedly.

"With any luck Quince and his boss will be waiting for Bendix's wagons. There's not a whole lot of luck needed beyond that—and we know Plummer sent two of his men to Lewiston to run his swindle again."

They rode in silence, each lost in private thoughts. Before they knew it, the creek widened into a sizable river just below the roadhouse. Slocum slowed and signaled for Jane to dismount.

"We made better time than I thought," he said. "Might be we could pass some time before Bendix gets here."

"Pass some time? You mean what I think you do, John? That's mighty dangerous, this close to the shebang."

"Not if we keep our voices down and don't make too much noise."

"You continue to surprise me, John," she said, reaching up to unbutton her blouse. "This might be real exciting." Jane froze, her blue eyes fixed on something behind Slocum. He saw the flash of fright on her face.

He spun around, went into a gunfighter's crouch and had his six-shooter out, cocked and aimed at the man holding two wood buckets. The man's eyes widened in surprise.

"Don't move, don't drop them, don't move a muscle," Slocum ordered.

"I—"

"Quiet," Slocum warned. He went to the man and checked to see that he had come to the stream alone to fetch the water.

"How many men are in the shebang? Other than Quince?"

"I can't s-say," the man stammered. "I just do as I'm told. I—"

Slocum slugged him. The man grunted, bent over a little, then crumpled to the ground.

"Tie him up," Slocum said to Jane, not waiting to see if she obeyed. "I've got to be sure we weren't spotted."

"John, wait!"

Slocum was already halfway to the rear of the shebang.

Four of Quince's men sat around, rifles leaning against the wall beside them. They played poker and paid no attention to him as he went to the stable and ducked inside. Two horses were still saddled. Slocum thought he recognized one as belonging to George Plummer, but he couldn't be sure. He made his way through the stable and assured himself only the horses were inside.

Carefully barring the double doors from the inside, Slocum crawled through a high window in the tack room and dropped outside. As he hit the ground, he heard a warning go up. He fell flat on his belly, six-shooter ready to take out the first man who opened fire on him.

Then Slocum realized the alert was for Clint Bendix and the wagons. Bendix had made good time up the rocky, steep road. Getting up, Slocum went to the corner of the barn and waited.

"Come on in and wet your whistles," called Quince to Clint Bendix. "We'll show you real hospitality."

Bendix kept his new hat pulled down to shade his eyes and had a bandanna up to hide his face. He coughed, brushed off a cloud of dust from his coat and jumped down.

"That's mighty hospitable of you," Bendix said, looking away as Quince came out.

Slocum knew from experience what would happen next. And it did.

"Thanks for bringing my merchandise out here," Quince said. "You see, I got receipts for all the goods in your wagon."

"What? You can't. This is all mine! I paid for it and shipped it this far," protested Clint Bendix.

"These receipts say different. You're a thief, but I ain't gonna tell Marshal Watkins over in Orofino about it, if you and your muleteers just start walkin'."

"You're wrong. Those papers are forgeries. There's no

way you could know what I'm packing," protested Bendix.

"Boys, show 'im how wrong he is," ordered Quince. His men, all armed with rifles, moved to pull back the tarps. "See?" Quince said, not bothering to look. "That there crate is full of fancy food from San Francisco. Cookies and other baked goods done by them Chinee bakers."

"No, it's not," said Bendix.

"Open the box and show 'em *my* fine merchandise," Quince ordered. He turned when his man gasped.

"Boss, there's nuthin' but rocks in the box. Plain old rocks!"

"And you got rocks in your head if you thought you could keep up this swindle," said Bendix. "You went to the well once too often!" He grabbed Quince and knocked the man to the ground.

Then the flurry of motion all around confused and disoriented the road agents. The tarps in the wagons were cast back and Sheriff Allen with four deputies and eight more posse members had their rifles and shotguns leveled and ready to cut down any outlaw foolish enough to fight.

Guns dropped and hands lifted for the azure Idaho sky. And Clint Bendix whaled the tar out of Quince, until Sheriff Allen pulled the teamster off.

"That'll do, Bendix. I got him now. You're under arrest, Quince, you and all your boys."

"Marshal Watkins—" sputtered Quince. He spat blood from his mouth. Bendix had cut his lip and bloodied his nose.

"I'll be looking in on the good marshal when I get you boys locked up. Reckon Watkins would like the cell next to yours?"

"Boss!" shouted Quince.

This alerted Slocum in time to see two men race from the rear of the shebang. He stepped out and fired, hitting the leading man. The outlaw tumbled to the ground but wasn't injured badly enough not to return fire. Slocum had to duck back to avoid a hail of bullets.

"It's Plummer!" shouted Slocum to the sheriff. "He's making a run for it out the back!"

Slocum tried to get around to the front of the barn, where he heard someone frantically trying to open the double doors. He was glad he had barred them from the inside. Slowing Plummer's escape gave the lawman time to tie up Quince and the others and then bring guns to bear on the real leader of the road agents.

The rattling stopped suddenly and Slocum worried Plummer had hotfooted it across the meadow, heading for the alders some distance away. Slocum swung around the corner and almost got plugged by the outlaw he had winged. Slocum fired several more times and finally hit the owlhoot.

The thunder of hooves told Slocum that Plummer had gotten into the barn and had used a side door to get away. He ran to the far side of the barn and snapped off a shot. He missed. Then his hammer fell on an empty chamber.

"John, he's getting away!" Jane Garson rode up, struggling to keep her roan under control. "There he goes!"

Slocum jammed his empty six-shooter into his holster, turned and grabbed at the reins of her horse. The roan tried to buck, but Slocum held it firmly and kept the mare's head down.

"The horse! Let me have your horse," he ordered. Slocum was pleased that Jane didn't argue. She slid her leg over the horse and slid off to the right as Slocum mounted from the left. In the saddle, he reached down for the saddle sheath and found she hadn't brought a rifle.

"Here, Slocum, take this!" Sheriff Allen tossed him a six-gun. "Go get the varmint!"

Slocum shoved the sheriff's Colt into his belt, bent low and let the roan have its head. The horse shot away as if it had been goosed. Plummer had a bit of a head start, but Slocum's horse was a real champion when it came to speed.

He'd overtake George Plummer or know the reason.

21

Slocum got the lay of the land as he rode, his sense of direction telling him that Plummer was making a beeline for Paradise. Whether Plummer was responsible for the city's existence or had simply taken over something that already existed didn't matter much to Slocum. If Plummer reached Paradise, he'd have his sanctuary until the sheriff got enough cavalry units out to enter the passes and surround the town.

As he rode, Slocum got an uneasy feeling about the territory. He slowed and took a few minutes to study his back trail. Hoping for the best, he waited until he saw that the riders weren't part of Sheriff Allen's posse. They had left their horses in Lewiston in favor of hiding in the wagons, rightly thinking Quince and his men would be hard-pressed to escape. That worked against them pursuing Plummer.

And the men behind him weren't lawmen. Slocum doubted they had been at Quince's shebang, but it hardly mattered where they came from. They were outlaws intent on reaching Paradise, just like their boss. Slocum counted the best he could and came up with eight men, all armed and undoubtedly nervy if they had robbed a bank or wagon train.

He looked from them back toward the towering Bitter-roots where Plummer headed. Getting caught between the Paradise sentries and the road agents behind him wasn't anything Slocum hankered for, but he had no choice. He had to catch Plummer before he got away.

Slocum drew his horse around. The roan pawed at the ground, as if it were ready to gallop all day long. Slocum let it run. The horse seemed as anxious to escape something as Slocum was to overtake Plummer. The outlaws behind him posed an added danger, but speed was on Slocum's side.

He caught sight of Plummer after twenty minutes of headlong gallop interspersed with quick walking and then trotting. The horse was indefatigable, and this equine stamina spelled Plummer's doom. Slocum caught him a half dozen miles short of what he suspected was an entry point to the valley cradling the outlaw haven.

Plummer heard Slocum coming and drew his six-shooter. He shot awkwardly over his shoulder. Slocum never slowed. It would be a lucky shot to hit him at this range. Let Plummer exhaust his supply of ammo. But Slocum reconsidered as he rode the outlaw down. The gunshots would alert both the sentries and the road agents trailing behind. Until now those eight desperadoes hadn't known anyone was nearby.

When Plummer's gun came up empty, Slocum put on an added burst of speed. He worried that the roan might be tuckered out after its exertions, but the valiant horse responded without hesitation. Closer and closer he came to the outlaw, until they were only yards apart.

"Give up, Plummer, give up or I'll shoot you out of the saddle!" Slocum drew the six-shooter the sheriff had given him. He cocked and aimed it. Shooting from horseback was always chancy, but at this range Slocum knew he could hit Plummer or his horse—and Plummer saw it, too.

"I give up!" cried the outlaw. Plummer let his exhausted horse come to a halt. He put his hands into the air. "You got me, but I can make it worth your while. I've got gold. Lots of it!"

"I don't want your blood money," Slocum said. He remembered the death and destruction Plummer had left in his wake. Robbing Clint Bendix and the other packers and miners was bad enough, but the deputy had been shot and the two turncoats in the Lewiston jail had been brutally slaughtered. It had been a stroke of luck that no one else in Lewiston had died in the fierce fire Plummer had set to get Luke Latham out of the calaboose.

"Anything, I'll give you anything you want. I run an entire town. It's up there in the mountains. Women? I can get you the prettiest ones in Idaho Territory!"

Mention of women set Slocum's mind to running in a different direction.

"Get down," he ordered the outlaw.

"Don't shoot me. Please."

Slocum dropped to the ground and fished through the saddlebags, hoping Jane actually had brought the papers. He found a thick sheaf and pulled them out. A quick glance convinced him these were the divorce papers she'd had drawn up by the Lewiston lawyer.

"Sign these," Slocum said, thrusting the papers toward Plummer. The outlaw looked confused.

"What is it? A confession? You got me fair and square. There's no reason for me to sign anything." Plummer was getting his nerve back, and Slocum knew why. They were closer to the gap leading into Paradise than he had thought. Plummer reckoned a guard would see what was going on and bring out a passel of outlaws to gun Slocum down.

Slocum worried less about that than he did about the

eight gunmen on his tail. They headed for this same pass
and would be in sight within a few minutes.

"You can't read?" asked Slocum. He saw that Plummer
couldn't. "These are divorce papers."

"From Jane?" Plummer looked confused. "You rode me
down and all you want is for me to sign?"

"You can write your name, can't you?"

Plummer nodded. He looked a powerful lot more confident now.

"Then sign. Here." Slocum had fished out a stubby pencil from the saddlebags and tossed it to Plummer.

"You could have been rich," Plummer said. "If this is
all you want, then I'll oblige. I'm glad to be done with
that bitch." He chewed on his tongue as he carefully
signed his name. When he finished, he glanced up at Slocum. "Now what? You going to take me in for the reward?"

Slocum felt the faint quaking in the ground under his
boots. The eight riders were getting closer. He might try
to sneak away with Plummer as a captive, but he doubted
the outlaw's horse would last too long if it came down to
a real race. Plummer's horse wobbled and looked as if it
would collapse to the ground at any instant. As strong as
Slocum's roan was, riding double wouldn't work, not with
a prisoner.

"I ought to plug you," Slocum said. Fear flashed in
Plummer's eyes, then it faded.

"You wouldn't last five minutes if you did," Plummer
said. He jerked his thumb over his shoulder in the direction of the mountain pass. Four men wended their way
out of the mouth and were closing in on their boss.

"I might not last five minutes if I don't," Slocum said.

"Get the hell out of here. If those papers are all you
wanted, I don't want to waste a bullet on you."

Slocum stuffed the divorce papers into the front of his
shirt and vaulted into the saddle. He knew he had very

little time. As satisfying as it would be to gun down George Plummer, Slocum knew both bands of outlaws would be after him in a flash. Letting Plummer live might slow them down a few seconds while they asked for explanations—or Plummer might actually order them all into Paradise. He had to know the law was after him because of Sheriff Allen's raid on the shebang.

Plummer just didn't understand the full extent of it yet.

Slocum rode parallel to the mountains and then angled away, thinking he would circle the eight road agents behind him and report back to the sheriff. And give Jane her papers.

The outlaws from Paradise gave Slocum a merry chase, but he managed to lose them by sundown. The ride back to the shebang was almost leisurely after all he had been through that day.

"There, it's final," Jane said. She dusted off her hands as if she had been working. "George Garson's out of my life forever!"

Slocum's mind had drifted to other matters during the court proceedings but now returned to her small victory. The circuit judge had come to Lewiston and set up court. Jane had been so insistent that everyone agreed to let her be the first case heard. Now her divorce from Plummer was final.

"You're a free woman," Slocum said.

Her shoulders slumped. "George is still free, too. That irritates me. He ought to swing for all he's done. Look around and tell me that's not so!"

Lewiston was still in the throes of rebuilding, but the charred timbers remained and the stench would linger for months. What benefited the town as much as anything was a new gold find near Orofino. Miners by the score came through on their way to the goldfields, all needing supplies and finding Lewiston a convenient stopping-off spot before they got down to serious work.

As usual, the first buildings renovated were the saloons and cathouses, but the hotel was almost rebuilt and four new stores alongside were open for business. The one building that everyone in town had insisted be rebuilt was the town jail. Sheriff Allen now had a lockup twice the size of the one that Plummer had burned down.

"It's been a couple weeks since the raid on Quince's shebang," Slocum said. "The sheriff's arrested Quince and all his men and caught a couple more trying to rob miners on their way to Orofino."

"And Marshal Watkins is locked up, too."

"That leaves Orofino without any law. It's a wide-open town."

"But George is still at large. I want to see him before that judge—for real crimes!"

"What he did to you counts as a real crime," Slocum said.

"You're so sweet, John."

That characterization bothered Slocum more and more. Jane had come to look at him with dewy eyes. He was already getting the urge to move on, but there was one last chore that needed doing.

"Bendix!" he shouted, waving to his friend. Clint Bendix had ten wagons now, some given to him by the merchants of Lewiston and Orofino to ensure a constant supply of the goods they needed most. Bendix had made two trips to Coeur d'Alene already. But this time he had brought a special cargo.

"Hey, Slocum, you ole polecat. I was wonderin' if you'd moved on yet." Bendix's eyes darted from Jane to Slocum and back. She hadn't seemed to notice what Bendix had said—and assumed.

"Today's when they arrive," Slocum said.

"What's going on?" asked Jane.

"You worried that Plummer would get away. Sheriff Allen knew he couldn't tackle the entire town of Paradise by himself so he's been waiting for the Army to show up. Three companies of infantry and two of cavalry are knockin' on Plummer's door right about now."

"They're marching on Paradise? That's wonderful!"

"We can have a front-row seat for what I think'll happen. Are you up for it?" Slocum asked.

"You kin ride with me, if you like," Bendix offered.

"How can I refuse?"

Slocum fetched the roan mare that he had taken such a fancy to. The spirited animal was more than Jane could handle easily, but for Slocum it was about perfect. She rode alongside Clint Bendix in the driver's box. Together, they made their way toward Orofino but took the turnoff when they reached Quince's shebang.

"What's going on here?" Jane asked. Her blue eyes widened as she saw the Army bivouac. Guards marched their rounds and officers' gold braids shone in the bright sunlight.

"They set up their headquarters here for the campaign against Paradise," Slocum said. "When the Army learned so many of the residents of that hideout were wanted for crimes against the government, they took a real interest in listening to Sheriff Allen."

"Where's the sheriff?" asked Jane.

"He'll be along shortly, 'less I miss my guess," Bendix said. He fastened his reins around the brake, then helped Jane to the ground.

"Why'd you bring an empty wagon out here?" Jane asked. "There's so much you're not telling me. I—"

Slocum wasn't paying any attention. He wished he had been riding with the sheriff when he led the Army through the pass into Paradise, but being here as they brought in the prisoners was about as good.

"There must be a hundred men the soldiers are marching at gunpoint," Jane exclaimed.

"Could be," Slocum agreed, but his keen eyes worked

to pick out particular men in the horde of prisoners. His heart beat a little faster when he spotted Luke Latham. The man hobbled along and had his arm bandaged. His face was bruised and battered, but other than these superficial wounds he was in good shape.

His neck would stretch just fine after the judge back in Lewiston got down to conducting the serious trials.

"Sheriff," greeted Slocum. "I see you were successful."

"Never been much of a supporter for the Army. They were always a pain in the ass, demanding and never giving, but this time they earned their pay. Three hundred infantry marched into Paradise after we took out the sentries on four different passes into that valley. Then their cavalry patrolled the countryside picking up the ones that got away. We got you to thank for letting us know about the tunnel under the bank. A few of them varmints would have escaped if we hadn't looked for the openings outside town."

"All of them?" asked Jane. "Did you get *all* of them?"

"Yes, ma'am," Allen said, knowing what she meant. "I personally caught him. He was one of them trying to escape using the tunnel."

George Plummer shuffled up, a soldier with a bayonet prodding him along. He started to say something when he saw Jane, but the soldier kept him moving to the wagon Clint Bendix had brought.

"The wagon!" Jane cried in delight, clapping her hands. "You drove out so you could move them all back to town for trial!"

"That's it," Bendix said. "They've got so many, I might have to make a second trip. Consarn it." He smiled ear to ear at the notion of having so many outlaws to cart off to prison.

"We'll still have road agents preying on miners and other travelers, but they won't have a place to hide now,"

Allen said. "Slocum, when you get back to town, you've got a fair reward coming."

"I didn't catch them, Sheriff," Slocum said.

"Your map of all the passes into Paradise saved lives, and that sketch you did of the town helped us round them up without too much lead being exchanged."

"The reward for George Plummer belongs to Jane," Slocum said.

"Won't argue with that," Sheriff Allen said. "Get down in that wagon," he bellowed. "Roll 'em out! Back to Lewiston!"

"You don't have to give me the reward on George's head," the raven-tressed woman said.

"After all the trouble he's put you through, you deserve something."

"As do you, John," she said with her bright eyes glowing.

"The Army's breaking camp and moving on. Their job's done," Slocum said. "There's no reason not to see if there's a spare room in the shebang."

There was.

Watch for

SLOCUM AND THE CIRCLE Z RIDERS

293rd novel in the exciting SLOCUM series
from Jove

Coming in July!

LONGARM

Explore the exciting Old West with one of the men who made it wild!